Quinn looked down at his briefs. "Sure, I do. As a matter of fact, I usually sleep naked. You just got lucky today."

"Lucky!" Sara exclaimed. "How dare you!"

"Hey, listen, lady. I don't remember inviting you into my bedroom, but since you're here, you'll have to take me as I am."

"I don't have to take you at all, Mr. Tucker. And like it or not, you start work today. Unless you have any problems I don't know about."

He did have a problem. He sighed. Faced with the idea of hard labor, he toyed with the idea of mentioning his tender rib cage.

It was the determined look in Sara's eyes that stopped him. She'd paid for his time. It was as simple as that. For the next twenty-six days, she owned him.

Dear Reader,

Another star appears in the American Romance
constellation this month as we introduce another
new writer to the series—Mollie Molay.

I first talked to Mollie days before the big quake
that hit Northridge, California—Mollie's home. In
fact, she did revisions to the manuscript right
through the earthquake! Mollie started writing years
ago when, as a going-away present, her co-workers
gave her an electric typewriter. Since then, she's
gone on to become president of the Los Angeles
Romance Writers of America. A part-time travel
agent, Mollie spends her spare time volunteering;
she's grateful for her good fortune and wants to give
back to those around her.

We hope you enjoy Mollie Molay's debut story,
From Drifter to Daddy, and all the Rising Stars
coming to you in the months ahead, only from
American Romance.

Sincerely,

Debra Matteucci
Senior Editor & Editorial Coordinator
Harlequin
300 East 42nd Street
New York, NY 10017

Mollie Molay

FROM DRIFTER TO DADDY

Harlequin Books

TORONTO • NEW YORK • LONDON
AMSTERDAM • PARIS • SYDNEY • HAMBURG
STOCKHOLM • ATHENS • TOKYO • MILAN
MADRID • WARSAW • BUDAPEST • AUCKLAND

To Justin and Nicholas for giving me Jase.
And to Ann, Aline, Betty, Joan, Risa Lee and Linda
for the countless Sunday mornings of good advice,
bad jokes and good food.
You are all more than friends.

ISBN 0-373-16560-9

FROM DRIFTER TO DADDY

Copyright © 1994 by Mollie Molé

Printed in U.S.A.

Chapter One

She was a woman dressed as a man, but there was no hiding her small waist, long legs and small, firm breasts that strained against her thin cotton shirt. Her curves, packed into tight-fitting jeans, were interesting too, and a dead giveaway.

She was also the only interesting sight he'd seen in three days of staring out of the jail's narrow window.

Two small children trailed her as she disappeared around the corner of Juniper, California's, adobe brick jailhouse. He strained to see more of her, but he was too late. Frustrated, he cursed his stupidity at getting himself arrested.

Restless, Quinn paced the small room. After three days in the eight-foot-by-ten-foot cell, he was ready to climb the walls. His whole life had been on the go. He couldn't stand to be confined. Having only Sheriff Cable for company hadn't helped matters, either. The man was incapable of listening to reason, and was responsible for the numerous bruises that covered Quinn's body. The fact that Quinn had gotten in a few good punches of his own when he'd been arrested was cold comfort, considering he'd landed in jail for thirty days.

Quinn froze at the gloating sound of Sheriff Cable's voice as he came down the dark, narrow aisle to Quinn's cell. The blonde he'd admired through the jail's window was with him.

"Well, Ms. Martin, there he is, just like I said. He's not much, but he's yours if you want him."

Straightening, Quinn tore his gaze away from the blonde and glared at the sheriff. "What do you mean, I'm hers?"

"Now see here, Tucker. Back off. Judge Andrews has decided to change your sentence to a work-furlough program."

"Work-furlough program! No one told me anything about a work-furlough program. What made the eminent judge change his mind?"

"You're costing the taxpayers money, that's why. No use having you here eating your head off and stirring up trouble."

"Eating my head off, am I? I haven't had a decent meal since I got unlucky enough to meet up with you!"

"That's enough out of you. You're damn lucky that Ms. Martin is thinking of paying your fine and letting you work for her," the sheriff blustered. "Lord knows why anyone would want you, with your record. If she agrees, you're hers for twenty-seven days. Good riddance, I say."

"What fine? The judge said he wouldn't let me go with a fine because I hit a law officer. He must be rewriting the law as he goes along."

"That's enough out of you. You got to go with Ms. Martin, and that's that!"

"She can have me when hell freezes over!"

Quinn's gaze locked with the blonde's, and he saw the doubt that clouded her coffee-colored eyes. He didn't care. He wasn't interested in going anywhere with her, anyway. Until he took a second look.

High cheekbones lent her face a delicate look, but from the condition of her worn clothing, he could tell she was used to hard work. Her skin was tanned from being in the sun.

He took in her long blond hair, tied back with a red ribbon. When she blew away the small tendrils that straggled across her forehead and licked her lips in a nervous gesture, his eyes widened. Until he noticed the two small children clinging to her legs.

Quinn sighed. The lady was married and he was behind bars. It was a hell of a combination and did nothing to soothe his impotent anger at being at Cable's less-than-tender mercy. Tense with resentment, he crossed his arms and waited to find out what she was doing there gazing at him as if he were a parrot in a cage.

The kids hung on to her pant legs, staring at him as though they expected him to jump through the jail cell bars and attack at any moment. Their identical coffee-colored eyes, shared by the blonde, were clouded with fear. Hell, he wasn't out to scare little children, although he probably looked fearsome with three days' worth of stubble and his shabby clothes. He forced himself to relax and lounged back against the iron frame of the bunk beds. Arms folded across his chest, he waited to see what the odd trio was going to do next.

His name was Quinn Tucker. That was all Sara Ann Martin knew about him, except that he was in jail for disturbing the peace and was available for "hire" if she was willing to pay his fine. He was the man she was looking for.

Troubled, she gazed at him. He was more than six feet tall, with the lithe body of an athlete. Ebony curls framed a rugged face darkened by the shadows of a growing beard. There were bruises on his forehead and above one eye. He had a sensual mouth, marred only by a cut at one corner of his lips. His torn and buttonless white shirt was open to his waist. Blue-and-yellow bruises showed under the mat of black curls that covered his chest.

Sara blushed as she caught herself following the curls to where they ended in a vee at the waistband of his worn jeans. She forced herself to meet his gaze. His hazel eyes glinted with anger, and something else she couldn't identify, even as they swept her from head to toe. He looked strong as a wild stallion, and just as angry.

She couldn't stop herself from staring at him. With his beard and his bruises, there was an aura of danger that clung to him. Even if he was hers for the asking, maybe she ought to reconsider. Common sense warned her to take the children and leave, but she needed cheap labor and she needed it now. Ignoring the sixth sense that was sending warning signals clanging through her body, she gritted her teeth and nodded.

"He'll do, Sheriff Cable. I'll take him."

The prisoner pushed away from the bed frame. The repressed anger on his face stopped the sheriff in his tracks as he was about to put the key in the cell door.

"I'll do for what?" the prisoner asked, eyeing her. The children whimpered at the tone of his voice, but he was obviously too angry to care. He moved to the door. In a voice cold as steel, he snarled, "Lincoln freed the slaves. What does *she* think she's going to do with me?"

Sara grabbed the children's shoulders and stepped back.

"Hold on there, Tucker," the red-faced sheriff admonished. "Better ease off before Ms. Martin changes her mind. Judge Andrews has agreed to let you work off your sentence by giving her a helping hand on her ranch—on one of those newfangled work-furlough programs. After she pays your fine, that is." Cable shot Quinn a malevolent look. "You ought to be grateful not to have to spend the next month in here with me." The threat in the official's voice was clear.

Quinn's cold gaze swung back to the blonde. The set look on her face spelled trouble. He was used to trouble all right, but somehow he couldn't see spending the next twenty-seven days paroled in her custody. Damn it, he was used to calling the shots. From the look on her face, he could see she was determined to be the caller.

The idea of being up for sale and bought by a woman was degrading and an affront to the little dignity he had left. He clenched his fists in frustration. His angry gaze swung from the blonde to Sheriff Cable. It was a case of the devil, in the guise of the barrel-chested sheriff, or the deep blue sea.

Hell, it wasn't being in jail that got to him. He'd been in jail before. It was being farmed out to a hostile woman that got under his skin and reminded him of his childhood and the years spent in foster homes, his presence barely tolerated.

One thing he did know, it would be a cold day in hell before he'd let himself be put to work like a mule. Once they were out of this hellhole, he'd find a way to get lost. He eyed the stern-faced woman. She didn't look as if she had what it would take to stop him, not with those two kids dogging her footsteps.

Well, he decided after a brief hesitation, he could run real fast when the occasion called for it. Maybe this was the occasion, he thought as he picked up his denim jacket. Maybe he was about to get lucky, after all. "Okay. I'll go with her."

He heard a smothered sigh of relief. The blonde must have been desperate enough to hire the devil himself, if she wanted him. He waited for her to back away from the door before he followed the sheriff. He could hear her murmur soft words of reassurance as, out of the corner of his eye, he saw her take a child by each hand as she trailed after them.

Sara liked the way Quinn Tucker walked: long, sure strides. He held himself ramrod straight, never glancing back to see if she had joined the parade into the sheriff's office. She was willing to bet there wasn't an unsure bone in his body. Good, she thought. He didn't look as if he would be scared off by what she had in store for him.

It took only a few moments for her to hand over the bail money and sign for Quinn's release into her custody.

"Buy a lot of cheap labor this way, do you?"

She whirled on him. "That's enough! You have a debt to pay to society, and as far as I'm concerned, I'm society. At least, for twenty-seven days. Keep a civil tongue in your head. There are children here!"

Conscious of his narrowed, angry gaze on her every movement, she found herself shaking by the time she gathered the children to her and led the way out of the jail door.

She saw Quinn blink and shade his eyes when he hit the brilliant noon sunshine. Three days in the darkness of the jail cell had undoubtedly made his eyes sensitive to light. A grimace of pain crossed his face as he ignored the impatient clearing of her throat and hesitated in the doorway while he became accustomed to the glare.

The dusty street, kept unpaved by the town council to make Juniper resemble a frontier town, shimmered in the sunshine. The wooden sidewalks were empty. Even the tourists who came to enjoy the historical town had the good sense to run for cover from the heat. But not her; she had important things to do.

Her parolee shrugged. "Another rotten day," he muttered, "in a string of rotten days."

But at least he followed her down the street.

Her old pickup truck was parked in front of the town's general store. A stack of grocery boxes sat waiting to be loaded into the flatbed. She saw the man gaze around the empty streets.

"Looking for something?"

"I was hoping to spot your husband so we can talk things over man to man."

"Mr. Tucker." She waited until she had his reluctant attention. "There is no husband. Please load the truck so we can get out of here." She drew a child to her side and pointed to the boxes. "I've wasted enough time."

Her voice was tight, whether from anger or fear, Quinn didn't know. But he was going to find out before the day was through.

At her gesture, he silently heaved the boxes into the truck and stood back. "Where's the man in your family?" He was surprised to see her bite her lower lip.

"Here," a small voice piped up. "I'm the man of the family, right, Aunt Sara?"

"You are?" Quinn inspected the boy. He was as slender as a young colt and just as spirited. Quinn glanced at the boy's aunt. She nodded. Her face was flushed, but there was a tender look in her eyes that spoke volumes as she gazed at the boy. Curious, he studied the young child. "How old are you?"

"Four and a half, almost five. I'm big, too. I can take care of everybody. I'm not afraid of anything." He clenched his small fist and flexed his muscle. "See how strong I am!"

"Kind of young to be the man of the house, aren't you?"

"Nah, just ain't tall enough. But I will be," he said bravely, as if daring Quinn to make something out of that remark.

Quinn felt a poignant tug. He knew from experience a blustering bravado could hide a lonely heart. Bending, he cupped the kid's arm with his hand. "Yes, I can see how strong you are. What's your name?"

"Jason McClintock, but most everyone calls me Jase. What's yours?"

"Okay, Jase. You can call me Quinn."

"His name is Mr. Tucker, Jase," Ms. Martin broke in. "Remember what I told you about calling grown-ups by their first names."

"It's okay with me if he calls me Quinn," he said with a sidelong glance.

"It's not okay with me. Please get in the truck."

Quinn smothered his irritation at her brusque tone. He turned his attention to the second child, who still clung to the aunt's leg. "This your brother?"

"No." Jase grinned. "That's Katie. She's my twin. She don't talk much."

"I can see that." Quinn ignored the annoyed look on Ms. Martin's face and solemnly studied Jason McClintock's sister. When she drew back, he held out his hand. "Hello, Katie. You can call me Quinn." Silence. He sighed, "I guess it's Mr. Tucker to you, too. I'm nice to children and animals. You don't have to be afraid of me."

She put her hands behind her back and inched closer to her aunt.

"I was hoping we could be friends," he said to erase the look of fear in her face, but he was unprepared for her continued silence. Damn! He wasn't used to being around kids, and now he was going to spend twenty-seven days with a frightened little girl and her too-old-for-his-age brother.

"Okay, partners." He sighed. "Let's get going and you can show me the way to your..."

"Ranch," came the short rejoinder from the children's aunt. "Get in back."

"That won't be necessary. Just give me a minute to pick up my truck and I'll follow you."

"Follow me for how long? What do you take me for—an idiot?" She looked him straight in the eye, as if daring him to make something of that remark. "The truck's impounded until you work off your fine—to make certain you don't change your mind.''

Damn! He had intended to follow the pickup for a mile or two, and then swing away at the first opportunity. Of course, he would have sent Ms. Martin her money when he had it, but it looked as if he'd have to bide his time. "And my suitcase?"

"That, too. Get in back," she repeated, matching his angry expression. "I've got to get back to the Lazy M." She hesitated. "This is your last chance. I can call the sheriff and tell him you've changed your mind."

Quinn felt impotent anger sweep through him again. All he had been guilty of was stopping to rescue a fallen animal that had been hit by a car, and they were treating him as if he were a man on the FBI's most wanted list. If it hadn't been for that damned hardheaded sheriff pushing him around, he'd never have punched the guy out. The fool had every blow coming, and Quinn wasn't sorry for any of it.

Sure, he'd spent some time drifting around the country and winding up in a county jail a time or two. Mostly for keeping the wrong type of company. Yeah, not to forget the time he once delivered a package for a friend that turned out to be some pretty strong stuff. He'd gotten a six-month sentence and three years probation for that caper. But that had been when he was younger and still filled with anger. He'd been clean for some time now. This trip to jail and the sentence to slavery was the last straw. Maybe somebody up there was telling him he had to put a lid on his temper.

He was tempted to call her bluff, but he knew he'd never get out of town if he got himself locked up again, not with his record. The way his luck was going, he'd probably get another thirty days under Sheriff Cable's gentle care. Biting back his frustration, he heaved the remaining boxes of groceries into the truck and silently followed.

"I'll get in back with him, Aunt Sara!" Jason struggled to reach the metal step at the back of the truck.

"No!" Sara took a step forward to stop him.

Quinn shot her a cold look and thrust a helping hand toward the boy. "What's the matter, afraid that he's not safe with me?" The answer showed in her eyes. "I may be guilty of arguing with the sheriff, but that's all. I never deliberately hurt anyone in my life and I'm not about to start now."

Jase's aunt stepped back and her expression turned uncertain. "Go ahead, Jase, but sit very quietly, and don't hang over the side." She moved to the driver's door of the truck. "And don't bend the man's ear any more than you can help."

Determined to find a way to get the situation back under his control, Quinn waited until she got into the truck. He'd keep the kid busy talking while he watched the road and for a chance to escape later on.

"Come on, Jase," he invited as soon as the truck started moving. "Tell me all about yourself. Where's your mother?"

"She's in heaven."

"And your father?"

"Don't know. He left when Katie and me was born. Mom said he had important things to attend to. I guess they were more important than Katie and me, 'cause he never came back."

The matter-of-fact answer took Quinn's attention off the road. A quick glance told him Jase accepted his mother's passing and his father's desertion much better than Quinn had done when his own parents had turned him over to someone else to raise. Kids deserved more than a father who ran out on them and left them with an aunt who was desperate enough to hire a jailbird.

"Where does your Aunt Sara fit in?"

"She's my mom's sister. Aunt Sara used to live in Los Angeles, but now she just takes care of Katie and me." Jase sighed. "Aunt Sara says we have to start school in September, but I already know how to read and write some. I'd rather stay home and help out at the ranch."

Based on his own experience, Quinn knew Jase couldn't stay a little boy as long as he wanted to. He had to grow up like everyone else. Quinn only hoped the future would be kinder to the boy than Quinn's childhood had been to him. "There's more to school than reading and writing, Jase." When the child looked doubtful, Quinn reassured him. "You'll learn a lot of things that will be more of a help to your aunt when you grow older."

Jase didn't looked convinced. Quinn changed the subject. "Tell me what your aunt wants with me."

"I don't know." Jase offered a shy grin. "But I'm glad you're here. Aunt Sara needs someone grown-up to help on the ranch." He squared his little shoulders and moved over to snuggle against Quinn. Touched, in spite of himself, Quinn put his arm around Jase and pulled him close. The boy was like a puppy dog seeking warmth, and just as innocent in his search for affection.

"Aunt Sara's awful nice. She came to take care of us when Mom got sick. Me and Katie like her a lot."

Quinn thought for a moment. The genuine affection in the boy's voice was a fervent testimonial to his aunt. If Sara Martin was that good to her niece and nephew, she couldn't be all bad. Not that it made any difference. He didn't intend to stay around any longer than it took to find a way out of Juniper.

Pothole after pothole in the hard-packed dirt road repeatedly threw Quinn against the sides of the truck. Smothering a curse, he looked over his shoulder at the driver. She was looking through the rearview mirror and mouthing the words, "I'm sorry."

Quinn grimaced as he rubbed the shoulder that had been bruised in his fight with the sheriff. "Sorry, hell!" he muttered. If it hadn't been for Jase sitting beside him and taking hard knocks with him, he'd have figured she'd probably done it on purpose to break up the conversation he was having with her nephew.

They turned down a narrow road that dipped into a small valley. He settled back to check out the territory and immediately wished he'd paid more attention to where they were going before now. But the kid's chatter had distracted him. Apple orchards and small horse ranches stretched as far as his eye could see. By now, they were miles from Juniper—that let out walking to the highway on foot and hitchhiking down to San Diego as he'd planned. Once there, he had intended to look up old friends, find a way to get the charge dropped, and to hell with Judge Andrews and Sheriff Cable. Of course, he thought righteously, he would have returned the two hundred dollars Ms. Martin had paid for him as soon as he got a job.

His thoughts wandered back to the first time he'd seen her through the jailhouse window. Just thinking about the way she'd looked in her tight-fitting jeans made his body stir again.

Too bad she was off-limits.

The way his shoulder and his bruised ribs ached from resisting arrest, he knew he was going to remember his stay in Juniper long after he was finally able to leave for a kinder and gentler territory.

The truck drew up in front of an old weather-beaten gate. A wooden sign hung from the fence pole—they were at the Lazy M ranch. Quinn glanced over his shoulder to see Ms. Martin pointing to the gate. He groaned and started to scoot toward the foot of the flatbed.

"Never mind, Mr. Tucker, I'll get it!" Jase jumped from the truck and ran to open the gate. Quinn rubbed his sore shoulder and gratefully shook hands with Jase after he helped the boy back into the truck.

They drove another hundred yards, and stopped in front of a neatly painted green-and-white frame cottage. A porch, covered by morning glories, ran along its length. White- and peach-colored rosebushes grew by the steps, and a small flower bed, outlined with whitewashed rocks, looked as if someone cared. Soft white ruffled curtains framed the windows, and the mat in front of the door spelled WELCOME. A small tree house sat precariously on a limb of an ancient apple tree that shaded the yard. At the side of the house, there was a weather-beaten barn with a lean-to jutting out one side, a chicken coop and an empty corral.

Quinn eyed the house and its surroundings with approval. Someone had put a lot of effort into making the spread look good. From the looks of Ms. Martin, he was sure she'd done more than her share of the work.

Before he could drag his bruised body out of the truck, he was startled by the sound of the truck horn. After a moment, Quinn could hear someone shout *"Hola!"* An aged Hispanic came hurrying from behind the house.

The man sported a smile that spread from ear to ear as he reached into the cab, caught Katie up in his arms and hurried to the rear of the truck. "You bring the fertilizer for the garden?" he asked as he peered at the boxes. When he spied Quinn carefully sliding from the ancient vehicle, he set Katie down and reached to help him down. "You have trouble, *señor?*"

Quinn grimaced. "Much trouble," he said, nursing his aching shoulder and his bruised ribs. "I'll be okay in a week or two," he added facetiously.

"There's horse liniment in the barn." Sara Martin's voice was terse. "You'll be fine by morning."

"Horse liniment?" Quinn's scowl made his displeasure obvious. "I thought that was for horses." He gazed around the spread. "I don't see any horses."

Katie's face lighted up in a proud smile. "We don't have a horse, Mr. Tucker, but we have a mule."

Jase chimed in. "Yeah, his name is Spike. Mr. Ramirez uses him to plow the garden."

Quinn blinked. Of all the possible names for a mule, Spike was the most incongruous. "Lucky mule to have such nice owners," he offered, more to get the annoyed look off Ms. Martin's face than to amuse the children.

"Okay, kids, back to business." Sara gave him a distant look and continued. "Everyone grab something and bring it into the kitchen."

Not to be outdone by a couple of four-year-olds, Quinn groaned, hefted a carton and trailed after them to the house and into the kitchen. At Ms. Martin's silent gesture, he put the box on an old scarred pine table.

"Nice," he said as he gazed around the room.

She made some noncommittal sound and reached to put away a can in the cupboard.

Quinn looked away from the rise of her breast to the old black-and-silver four-legged stove that stood against the wall. When the can dropped from Sara's fingers, he caught it and put it on the well-scrubbed linoleum counter. "You know, my grandmother had a stove like that."

"You lived with your grandmother?"

"For a time. Not long enough." Her sudden look of pity angered him. He didn't need anyone's pity, let alone hers. He turned his back and surveyed the rest of the kitchen.

A vintage refrigerator pumped alongside the stove. The sink was porcelain, chipped with years of use. Whatever money had been put into bringing the house into the twentieth century, it was obvious that not much had been spent on the kitchen.

Memories stirred, and with them the anger and frustration he'd carried around with him for years. His grandmother's kitchen had been a cozy room that had spelled home and family, had made him feel secure and loved. She'd passed away when he was ten and that security had passed away, too. The rest of his childhood had been spent being shunted from relative to relative by parents too busy to want him around. He frowned. This kitchen would have gladdened his heart, too, if he hadn't been here on a command performance.

"Say, do I smell chocolate chip cookies?" he asked, as he forced his thoughts away from those unloved, unhappy years.

He glanced around the room. There was a cookie jar in the shape of a teddy bear on the corner of the sink. Willing to bet that there was a supply of cookies inside, he moved to find out.

"Nice place you've got here," he said, fighting memories. He lifted the top of the cookie jar. Sure enough, it was filled with chocolate chip cookies. "Homemade?" he called over his shoulder.

Sara lifted her head from the box of groceries. "Yes. You can have one, if you like."

"I'd like." Quinn helped himself to a cookie, and passed a couple to the twins who had joined him at the cookie jar. He surveyed the room. "You keep the place nice. How big is the house?"

"Three bedrooms and..." Sara stopped in mid-sentence. "Why?"

"Where do I sleep?" he asked hopefully. "Or do I have to go back to the jailhouse at night?"

When she hesitated, he added, "I sure could use a hot shower. The sheriff's hospitality didn't go that far." For a moment he was sure she would let him stay in the house, until he remembered she knew next to nothing about him and would be foolish to take a chance on having him in the house. The knowledge burned him even more.

"You sleep in the lean-to, with Mr. Ramirez. I asked Judge Andrews to let you remain on the ranch at night by assuring him you wouldn't hit the trail." At Quinn's impassive expression, she added, "If you're smart, you won't make a liar out of me."

Her gaze locked with his. Quinn swallowed his sharp retort. If ever there was a time to bite his tongue, it was now, before he raised any suspicions in her mind about his intentions.

THE LEAN-TO was a neat twelve-by-fourteen room added on to the vacant barn. A wooden bunk bed stood along each wall, a small table and two chairs between them. An electric lantern hung from the ceiling. One corner had been curtained off to form a closet. The open door suggested a small bathroom. Quinn sank down on a chair, shrugged off his jacket and wondered if he would be lucky enough to find modern conveniences in there.

Quinn grimaced. Even though he realized he was a convicted man in the lady's eyes, he sure could have used that shower and a decent bed. Instead he was relegated to a lean-to with the hired hand for company.

Wearily he rose and looked inside the tiny room. An empty washbasin and pitcher rested on a narrow stand. An old-fashioned commode with a chain hanging from the ceiling was the only other furnishings in view. Hell! he thought bitterly. The lady was asking too much. He wanted a warm shower and a shave badly enough to storm the house.

He strode to the door in time to meet Miguel coming in, carrying a bottle of liniment. The odor made Quinn's face blanch and his stomach heave.

"Miss Sara say you need this." Miguel offered him the bottle.

"No thanks, keep it for the mule. I need to wash up. Got any ideas, Miguel?"

"*Sí*, in the summer I wash out back, Mr. Quinn. In the winter, Miss Sara, she let me use the shower in the house."

"Great!" Quinn reluctantly gave up the idea of a hot shower. He was getting more frustrated by the minute. "And what do I do about a razor?" he said as he fingered his prickly beard. "Another day with this and I'll look like a prairie cactus."

"I have extra one, Mr. Quinn. Come, I show you."

"Thanks." Quinn's stomach growled. "I'm starved. I could eat a whole steer, myself. Where do we eat, Miguel? Out back with the mule?"

Miguel hesitated. "You joke, no? I eat with the family. Miss Sara say to come to lunch as soon as you are ready."

Quinn gave up. "I joke, yes," he said, knowing his humor was lost on the literal-minded man. "The joke's on me. All I wanted was some time for myself. I got time, all right. Twenty-seven days with the little lady who runs this place. And all for giving that stupid sheriff what he had coming."

At Miguel's shocked expression, Quinn told him the story about his arrest while he washed, shaved and got back into the shirt he'd been wearing too long. "I stopped traffic on the road coming into Juniper when I tried to rescue a horse that had been struck by a hit-and-run driver. The blasted sheriff took exception to my good deed, and wouldn't listen to reason."

"And the horse, *señor?*"

"Hell, I don't know. I was trying to convince the sheriff to let me get help to save the animal. He kept insisting that the horse was dead and demanded I move it. The man wouldn't listen to reason, and I guess I lost my temper."

"That is so sad, Mr. Quinn. The sheriff, he was wrong."

"Yeah." Frustrated, Quinn ran his hands through his hair. "Maybe I'm paying for the rest of my sins."

"Sins, *señor?*" Miguel crossed himself.

"Got into the wrong crowd when I was too dumb to know better, and did a few things I'm not too proud of."

At Miguel's shocked expression, Quinn snorted. "I didn't shoot anyone, if that's what you're thinking. Fooled around with drugs."

"And now, *señor?*"

"I thought I'd gotten smart enough to stay out of trouble, but I guess I didn't learn a hell of a lot. I'm here, but heaven knows what for. Anyway, the way things look, Ms. Martin can't afford to feed me, let alone to have paid my bail."

"You are right, Mr. Quinn. Miss Sara has little money and much big problems. That is why I make the garden, so that the children will have fresh vegetables to eat. Miss Sara says things will change soon."

"And you believe her?"

"I have been here for five years, *señor.* I work for Miss Sara's sister and her husband, *Señor* McClintock, before that. Much bad things happen." A dark frown creased Miguel's forehead. "Miss Sara, she try hard to keep the family together since Miss Amy die. The children love her, and she loves them, but it is not enough." He shook his head. "God will reward her. I pray for her every day."

"I don't know what your Miss Sara wants with me. But I'm going to find out."

Diana Palmer

Chapter Two

Sara came out the kitchen door carrying a frosted pitcher of lemonade and a bowl of potato salad when she saw Quinn make his way across the yard. She could tell from the purposeful way he strode toward her that he had something on his mind. His clothes were badly rumpled, out of place with his freshly shaved face and clean, shining black hair. His buttonless shirt was gaping open, exposing a broad muscular chest covered with damp, dark curls. She blinked, involuntarily caught up in a desire to reach out and touch those curls, to feel them twist around her fingers.

She was embarrassed by what she was thinking. It had been a year since she'd felt a man's warm, bare flesh against her own. A year since she'd been hungry for a man's arms around her, loving her. When her fiancé said goodbye, she thought she'd put desire behind her. To her dismay, it came to life when she caught sight of Quinn's golden flesh. He exuded repressed strength and a vitality that could deliver excitement.

She bit her lip. What kind of woman was she to be attracted to his sheer maleness? To a man who disliked her and who obviously wanted to see the last of her? A man she'd found in jail. She didn't know, but there was something about him that drew her, made her think he was more than just a hot-tempered hoodlum in spite of his looks. Maybe it was that air of self-assurance that clung to him, as if he were more used to giving orders than taking them.

Still, she told herself firmly, it really didn't make any difference who or what he was. He wasn't going to be around long enough for her to get involved with him.

Quinn halted in front of her. She took a deep breath to still the ache that had started in her middle and forced her eyes from the drops of water that slid down his throat to his bare chest. The spicy smell of soap wafted toward her.

"I have a proposition for you, Ms. Martin, one that you'll probably like much better than having me around for a few weeks."

The invitation she thought she heard in Quinn's voice was almost more than she could handle. Instinctively she raised her hand to slap him, to show him what she thought of him and his blatant attempt to cash in on his masculinity. When his eyes narrowed, she lowered her arm. She didn't know just what this man *was* capable of.

"Too bad you didn't wash your mind with soap when you washed your face," she said coldly. "I've been propositioned before. I'm not interested."

Quinn's eyes glinted with anger. "Just like a woman, jumping to the conclusion that I'm interested in you."

He was right, and he'd gotten to her in spite of her determination to show him who was in charge.

"Ms. Martin, you haven't heard this one before. I'm willing to pay you off a little at a time, if you'll just let me go."

The expression on his face told her he wanted to get as far away from her as possible. No doubt, the last thing he wanted was to tangle with Sheriff Cable again.

"Now, why would I want to do that?"

"I'm not what you need."

"I think you are."

He raised his hand to stop her objections. "You can use the money to hire someone who can really do you some good." He paused. "As a matter of fact, I don't even know what you wanted me to do for you, but I do know you'd be better off with someone else."

Sara's glance flickered to his open shirt. His chest rose and fell heavily with repressed emotion. For a long moment, the heaving, tangled, damp curls on his chest held her spellbound. She cleared her throat and forced her eyes to meet his. "I don't think I need to find someone else. Not while you still have the rest of your sentence ahead of you. Besides, you look as if you can handle the job adequately. I plan on putting you to work right away."

His face grew white, his jaw clenched as though he had difficulty restraining himself. It was a good thing he realized that losing his temper wasn't going to get him very far.

"Doing what?"

"Digging holes for fence posts."

"Digging—" He started to protest.

"Yes, digging holes."

"What do you think I am, anyway?"

"Hired labor."

"You didn't hire me, lady," he spit out between clenched teeth. "You bought me, and I don't take kindly to that. This is a free country."

"I'm sorry you feel that way. When I agreed to pay your fine, I was told you would do anything I wanted you to do."

"I—"

"What I want, Mr. Tucker, is for you to help dig some holes."

"What *I* want, Ms. Martin, is to get the hell out of here!"

Sara eyed her irate parolee. "Then why did you agree to the work-furlough program when you had no intention of keeping your side of the bargain? What made you stop in the middle of the road, anyway? And hold up traffic to boot?"

"Because that's where the horse was."

"The horse? Sheriff Cable didn't say anything about a horse."

"Doesn't surprise me in the least. I stopped to see if I could help a horse that had been struck by a car. I'm sure it didn't ask to be hit any more than I asked to be here."

"And I'm certain that poor excuse isn't the only reason you were put in jail."

Quinn sighed. "Why does everyone around here want to know my life's history?"

Under her steady regard, he shrugged. "I guess it was a little more than that. After I hit him a few times, he handcuffed me, stuffed me in his car and took me off to the local judge. I have a record, if you must know, and the sheriff found it when he checked with the authorities. But the only thing I'm guilty of this time is punching him out."

Quinn could feel his temper getting dangerously out of hand. Knowing she was right didn't help matters. His innate honesty challenged his conscience. He knew that even when he'd agreed to the arrangement, he'd hoped to get out of it some way. Instead here he was, caught in a web of unforeseen circumstances he was powerless to change.

His sense of fair play prodded him to make her another, better, offer. "Maybe you could talk to Judge Andrews, make him see reason. Tell him I'll arrange to pay you off. In fact, I'll throw in a little extra so you can call the Farm Bureau and get experienced help. In exchange, you get the sheriff to let me off the hook."

"I don't need experienced help to build fences."

Sara moved past him to a picnic table under the apple tree beside the kitchen. She set the bowl and the pitcher down and turned to face Quinn. His temper was showing, and she was ready for it. "If you have money to pay your fine, why didn't you offer it when you had the chance? If you had, the judge might have canceled the work-furlough."

He shrugged. "In case you've forgotten, I wasn't told about a fine or a work-furlough program. Hell, I would have tried to raise bail but the judge wouldn't consider it. Said I hit a police officer and had a record. He'd have put me away for life if he could. I'm sure the money would have gone into Cable's pockets, anyway. Their attitude reeks of graft, and believe me, I know it when I see it."

"You had money and *I* had to bail you out of jail?"

"Well, not exactly. I'm sure I could have gotten it from a friend of mine if they'd let me." Quinn paused. "The way I see it, the judge and the sheriff were just getting even with me by keeping me in jail."

Sara scarcely smothered a smile. He looked strangely like Jase when the boy was trying to alibi his way out of trouble. "That's what happens to hot-tempered, spoiled—"

Quinn turned on his heel. "You may have bailed me out of jail, but I don't have to stand here and listen to your lectures." He was headed back to the lean-to when the kitchen screen door squeaked open and Jase and Katie came out carrying the rest of the picnic menu.

"We're going to have a picnic, Mr. Tucker!" Jase shouted. "Aunt Sara even took chocolate cupcakes out of the freezer for dessert!" He carefully put a plate of sandwiches on the picnic table and jumped up and down with excitement.

"So much for a hot meal," Quinn muttered under his breath as he turned back to join the group. If he hadn't been so damn hungry, he would have beaten a dignified retreat to the lean-to. Sheriff Cable's idea of meals had been sandwiches for breakfast, lunch and dinner. Right now, Quinn would have given a day's wages for a huge T-bone steak and all the trimmings.

Still, the ham and cheese sandwiches were surprisingly good, and his mood mellowed as he chewed. The lemonade was tart and cold, the salad just the way he liked it. Potatoes, eggs, onions and mayonnaise—no fancy pickles or red peppers to disguise the taste of those freshly boiled potatoes. Maybe there'd be real food for dinner. Even after he'd downed two sandwiches, he was still hungry. The chocolate cupcakes looked good. He saw Jase and Katie giggling as they sneaked their cupcakes before their sandwiches were finished.

Sara caught his hungry glance at the cupcakes. She held out the plate of sandwiches. "Another sandwich, Mr. Tucker?"

"Call me Quinn," he said sourly. "Under the circumstances, we might as well be informal."

A becoming blush rose over her face. Quinn recalled that Jase had said his aunt had lived in Los Angeles; for a big-city woman, Sara Ann Martin came across as an unsophisticated lady. In her boots and well-worn jeans, she looked as if she'd lived on a farm all her life. He glanced at her long, slender hands, hands an artist would have envied, even the way they looked now. Her nails were cracked, the skin scuffed. There was a purple bruise across the knuckles of one hand and an adhesive bandage on the other.

"What have you been doing to your hands, digging ditches?"

"How did you guess?" Hurriedly, Sara hid her hands in her pockets. "That's why I hired you." She eyed Quinn's hands. His were large and capable. There was a pale band across his right pinky finger where he'd worn a ring. She had no doubt that it had been confiscated by Sheriff Cable along with the rest of Quinn's belongings. "Your hands look as if you've done some hard work lately."

"Some."

"Then maybe you won't have a problem with digging ditches."

"Hey, I can do anything you can do."

"Oh no, you can't."

"Oh yes, I can," Quinn retorted. "We could keep this patter up all day, but if it's all right with you, I'd rather discuss my departure from this Garden of Eden."

"Twenty-seven days," Sara said evenly. "The sooner you accept that, the better off both of us will be."

"That's what you think!" Quinn rose to his full height, leaned across the table and glared down at Sara. "You're a hardheaded lady."

"Twenty-seven days, Mr. Tucker. You help me build fences, and *then* we'll discuss your departure."

"Are you asking me, or telling me?"

"Anyway you want to see it." She handed him the plate of cupcakes. "Here, try something sweet to curb that temper of yours. It won't be so bad. After all, I'll be working with you."

"Yeah," Quinn said dryly. "That ought to help a lot." If the lady thought a cupcake and the dubious comfort of her working alongside him would soothe the savage beast, she had another think coming.

He caught the wide-eyed faces of the twins as they followed the conversation between himself and their aunt. The last thing he wanted was to have them hear the argument going on. He'd heard too many of them as a boy growing up in homes where he wasn't wanted. "Why don't you kids go and play?" He watched as the children glanced at their aunt for permission before they ran off.

Quinn realized how angry he must have sounded and sat down. He decided to try again—quietly and logically.

"Why didn't you hire a local man instead of opting for a slave?"

"Don't be so melodramatic. You're not a slave. The truth is, I don't have enough money to pay minimum wage to anyone, even if I wanted to. You're not worth much, but you'll have to do."

"You sound as if you're one of those women who have it in for men."

Sara saw red. "Who do you think you are, anyway? For your information, I grew up in Juniper, and stayed long enough to learn most of the local men are like my missing brother-in-law, chauvinistic and lazy. I went away to college and stayed in Los Angeles to work, but I soon found men were no improvement there, either. I was engaged to a lovable happy-go-lucky guy whom I met at work. But when he found out I was given the children to take care of, it was the last I saw of him. Don't tell *me* anything about men!"

"I didn't intend to, ma'am. I just wondered if you have it in for all men, or is it just me?"

"I've known for a long time there weren't any men to be trusted. Not in Juniper, or anywhere else. At least with you, Quinn Tucker, I'll see to it that you get the job done and get out of my life."

Her voice trailed off as Quinn narrowed his eyes. She hadn't meant to sound so bitter, but there was something about him that made her defensive, even as she felt attracted to him. "Watch yourself, Mr. Tucker, or *I* might be the one who changes her mind about bringing you to the ranch."

"You mean I can still get out of here?"

"I know what you're doing. You're trying to anger me enough to let you go. It won't work. If I change my mind, it would only take a phone call to Judge Andrews and you'd be back in jail where you belong."

Quinn shrugged. "Sounds to me as if I'm not the only one with problems. This is some mess you've gotten yourself into."

"I wouldn't consider having to take care of Jase and Katie a mess. I promised my sister I'd take care of her children and protect their heritage, and I don't regret a moment of it."

"Maybe you ought to try living your own life," Quinn said, eyeing her. "With a knockout figure like yours and a face that belongs on a magazine cover, you sure are wasted on a dirt-poor ranch with only the twins and Miguel for company. You're kind of exiled out here."

At the way her body reacted to his frank assessment of her, and her chagrin at having told him more than she intended, Sara colored and jumped to her feet. She swept the empty dessert plate from the table with more force than necessary. "It may look like exile to you, but it's home to me. Not that I care what you think," she muttered under her breath as she made for the house. The screen door banged loudly behind her.

Quinn finished the last of his cupcake. He gazed idly at the neat but barren yard, the empty corral and the farm tools rusting in an open shed. There was the apple orchard, the kitchen garden and the few flowers that grew by the front porch of the house; nothing to indicate a working ranch.

So this was home, was it? No wonder Ms. Martin had to resort to indentured labor—there wasn't a sign of any activity that might have paid the rent, let alone a hired hand.

In a way, he felt sorry for her. She was a lot like him—strong-willed and stubborn. She had a temper of her own, too. Too bad she was fighting a losing battle in her attempt to make the ranch pay its own way. Keeping him around wasn't going to change anything.

The sheriff's impounding his truck and his suitcase was a low blow, too, but what could he expect from a judge who'd decided Quinn was guilty of assault and battery just because he had a record of prior arrests. The only good thing about the situation was that tomorrow was Sunday and he was going to get a day of rest before he had to start digging those damn holes.

Jobs had been scarce—a few days here and there, and he'd been on his way again. It was a good thing he didn't care for roots because he wasn't going to have a chance to grow any.

Quinn whistled a mournful tune as he contemplated the next few weeks and mentally cursed his own stupidity for landing in such a mess. Not that it should have surprised him any. The way things had been going for the past few months, it was about the only thing left that could have happened to him.

A sudden twinge reminded him of his bruised ribs. Right about now, a feather bed would be mighty welcome. Instead all he had to look forward to was a narrow cot in Miguel's shed and a shower he was going to rig up if it was the last thing he did.

Just as he rose to stroll back to the lean-to, Sara stormed out of the house. She thrust a man's shirt at Quinn. "Here, this one has buttons on it. Put it on and cover up."

SARA STORMED into the lean-to. When Quinn hadn't come in for breakfast, she knew he was still fast asleep. She'd show him who was the boss around here.

"Get up. The fence posts are waiting."

He groaned and burrowed deeper into the pillow. "I thought today was Sunday."

"What's the matter? Does the idea of honest physical activity bother you?"

"No indeed. It depends on what kind of physical activity you're talking about." Quinn rolled out of bed and brushed the sleep out of his eyes.

Sara gasped. "You don't have any clothes on!"

He glanced down at his Jockey shorts. "Sure I do. As a matter of fact, I usually sleep naked. You just got lucky today."

"Lucky! How dare you?"

"Hey, listen, lady. You barged into my bedroom, such as it is. I don't remember inviting you in, but since you're here, you'll have to take me as I am."

"I don't have to take you at all, Mr. Tucker."

He gazed at the flush that covered her cheeks and was rapidly spreading down to her neckline. Her breasts rose and fell rapidly under her cotton blouse as she stared at him. His body stirred. When he saw her eyes widen, he knew it was time to cover up before they both had something to regret.

"You'll have to wait a minute while I get dressed." He stepped into his jeans. Her eyes followed the hand that closed the zipper. When his hand paused, she glanced up into his eyes and blinked.

"Now, now, Ms. Martin. Just what did you have in mind?"

"Fence posts." Sara felt like a fool as she forced her mind off the man's body.

"Fence posts. Sure. Well, I'm used to hard work. It's just that the prospect of digging holes in the hot sun has no appeal for me whatsoever."

"Hard work?" Sara echoed. "Just what is it you do when you're not getting yourself arrested?"

He clamped his lips shut. He didn't want to tell her he had no permanent job, in fact didn't want one. That he couldn't stand staying in one place for very long and, furthermore, didn't want to tie up with anyone or anything. That he'd been that way for most of his life. As for getting arrested, yes, that too. Seemed as if every time he lost his temper, he wound up in some jail while they checked him out. That record of his had kept him in jail too often, too long.

Sara seemed to sense his reluctance to talk. "Never mind. It's really none of my business. I need you to dig ditches, period. So if there's anything else on your mind, forget it." As she turned to leave, she glanced at the shirt he'd put on.

Quinn followed her gaze. "Something wrong with this shirt, too?"

"Not at all. I just wondered if your bruises are healed."

Quinn's hands rose to the top button of his shirt. "Care to take a closer look?"

"No," Sara said firmly. "Healed or not, you start work today. Unless you have any other problems I don't know about?"

He did have a problem, and he was willing to bet that she did, too. He sighed. Faced with twenty-six days of hard labor, Quinn toyed with the idea of mentioning his tender rib cage. It was the determined look in her eyes that stopped him. Indentured labor or no, she'd paid for his time. She owned him—it was as simple as that. At least, until he found some way out of this mess. "Just some pain, but I'll get through it."

Quinn tore his eyes away from the spun gold that was Sara's blond hair. Its lush, shining texture made his fingers ache to lose themselves in its silken depths, to feel it sliding through his fingers. Too bad she kept her hair tied so neatly. It would look glorious blowing in the wind or spread across a pillow. The pictures his mind conjured up were so real he could feel his body stir again. He forced his thoughts to the matter at hand with difficulty. He wasn't here to create any more problems for himself. "Okay. When do we start?"

He was rewarded by a relieved glance. "I'm glad you're seeing it my way. Come on in and get some breakfast. I'll show you what I want you to do."

Outside, they were interrupted by Jase. "Aunt Sara, can we be excused? Miguel is going to show us the baby carrots and green onions that came up last night while we were sleeping!" His eyes swerved to Quinn. "Mr. Tucker?"

"Your aunt is going to be fine with me," Quinn assured him, realizing that the kid was asking for assurance.

Jase nodded. "Can we, Aunt Sara?"

"All right, but stay with Miguel until I come back!" Sara waved goodbye and brushed her hair away from her eyes. "They're such good children. I want to do so much for them."

Quinn gazed after the children. He'd never had or wanted kids of his own and wouldn't know what to do with them if he did.

"You don't happen to have any more clean clothes, do you? These are the only ones I have, and I'd hate to ruin them."

"Upstairs, in the house. First room on the left, but don't get any ideas about staying. There's some work duds in the closet. Take what you need." She eyed him critically. "You might get dirty where we're going. Better wait to shower and change again when we get back."

Quinn had difficulty in holding back a whoop of pleasure. A shower and fresh clothing! Life was good.

Ten minutes later, ignoring still-aching ribs, Quinn hopped into the passenger's side of the truck. He bit back a ready wisecrack when Sara slid in beside him. She'd exchanged her garments for some she obviously considered more expendable than the old clothing she'd worn before. Oversize trousers were belted at her waist, and boots covered her legs. No matter how practical she tried to be, she still looked utterly feminine and mighty desirable. Too bad she acted like a jail warden.

"How about the kids?"

"Miguel will watch them. He knows where I'm going, I told him this morning."

"And we're going..."

"Wait and see." Sara sighed as she started the engine. "There's so much work to be done, it's hard to know where to start."

They drove across a dry winding stream bed and down a dirt road, leaving a dust trail as they went. The dry, still air grew hotter as the sun rose. Flocks of chattering quail shot into the air as they drove by.

"Sure is hot." Quinn wiped perspiration from his forehead with the back of his hand. "Is it always like this around here?"

Sara took her eyes off the road, a worried frown on her face. "We're in a drought. It's dried up most of the water around here. Where do you come from, Mr. Tucker?"

"Here and there," he muttered vaguely. He'd been drifting so long, he scarcely remembered where he'd been, let alone knew where he was going.

By the time they turned into dry pastureland, Quinn was longing for the sight of water—any water. He was getting angrier at himself by the minute for losing his temper and getting into this mess instead of winding up camping in the mountains as he'd intended.

The truck skidded to a stop in front of a small stack of notched fence posts, another of split rails and a posthole digger. "Over there, where I left off." She pointed to a pole marked with a red ribbon similar to the one she wore in her hair. "See?"

"Fence posts." Quinn said dismally. "I was hoping you were just putting me on to get even with me. What do you need with fence posts?"

"To keep the horses in."

"You don't have any horses," he said automatically, remembering the empty corral.

"I know, but we will."

He slid gingerly out of the truck and winced when his feet hit the hard ground. As far as his eye could see, there was nothing moving except a family of rabbits that had disappeared into a grove of apple trees at the sound of the pickup's motor. "You don't need fences for your mule, do you?"

"No. But I figured I might as well start with fences before I advertised the Lazy M as an animal bed and breakfast."

"Animal bed and breakfast! What do you know about boarding horses?"

"I grew up here, and we had a horse when I was a kid."

"Hey, that's not the same thing. It was probably a pet. This would be for real. Currying horses is a hard way to make a living. I know, I've done it." Quinn gestured at the dry pasture. "I don't think there's enough grass around here to feed horses, anyway. Buying hay is going to be expensive."

"Could be, but I have to do something to make the ranch pay. I have to take care of the children."

"Maybe you should just try to find their father and make him pay up."

"I see Jase has told you about Richard McClintock. The man is worthless. I don't want him anywhere near the kids."

Quinn admired the lady's guts—but she sure wasn't realistic.

"Let's get started. You can start over here, right after the last post I put in. Dig a hole every ten feet for a fence post. We'll hang the rails later."

Quinn bit back a cuss word, shrugged and picked up the posthole digger. He'd never used one before, but if Sara Martin had been using one, then he could do it, too. If he didn't cut off a toe or two in the process.

He thrust the tool into a hole Sara had started, cursed under his breath and stomped on it.

"I thought these would be electric nowadays."

"Maybe, but I don't have the money to buy 'em. Keep trying. Here, let me show you."

When she grasped the pole, her breasts came in contact with his chest. The reminder that she was definitely a woman in spite of her odd attire sent a new wave of awareness through him. When she moved the instrument back and forth to send it deeper into the earth, her breasts under her cotton shirt moved, too. So did his body.

Feeling as if his manhood was in question, Quinn took the pole from her and went to work.

Chapter Three

A week later, Quinn was still digging holes, setting fence posts and hanging split wooden rails. His ribs were begging for mercy. So were his raw hands and his aching back. He was too proud to ask Sara to ease up on him, but right now he wanted a soft flat surface to rest on more than he'd wanted anything in his life.

It was his own fault. If he hadn't lost his temper and punched out a sheriff, he wouldn't be digging holes in dusty soil under a hot sun. He'd be camping out under an oak tree under summer skies, enjoying lazy days and lazy nights, and drifting on when the spirit moved him. As it was, he was on a work-furlough program with a jailer who had him working harder than that mule of hers.

He glanced over to where Sara searched for the boundary stones that marked off her property from the neighboring ranch. She was wearing that outlandish combination of work clothing again. Today, because of the intense heat, she'd tied the shirt at her waist and had left the top partially unbuttoned. Quinn covertly observed the curve of breasts and the flesh on her exposed trim waist and shifted uneasily as his jeans grew tighter.

Sunlight became Sara Martin, he thought as he leaned on the posthole digger to admire her. Her hair ribbon had fallen off, allowing silken golden strands to stir in the light breeze. He grinned as she repeatedly brushed them away from her face, only to have them fall over her coffee-colored eyes again. He definitely liked her better with her hair loose, he decided. It made her look sexy as hell.

He watched with interest as Sara bent over and backtracked, looking for the missing ribbon. Her blouse gaped at her throat, exposing her suntanned flesh. Another button on her shirt came undone as she straightened, the hair ribbon in her hand, revealing a lacy undergarment. Beneath her mannish clothing, Sara Martin was all woman—and then some. Knowing what she wore under her clothing made her figure more inviting than it had been the first time he'd glimpsed her through the jailhouse window.

When she raised her arms to tie back her hair, revealing an expanse of skin around her middle, he swallowed hard. In contrast to the tanned skin on her arms, her sculpted waist was pure white and inviting as sin. He couldn't tear his gaze away from its creamy expanse to save his life. It was then that Sara's glance caught his and, arms in midair, she flushed. He forced himself to look away, but not before she hastily rebuttoned her shirt and turned her back on him.

Her reaction pleased him. Beneath those mannish clothes, she was a flesh-and-blood woman. From what he'd glimpsed, one with a very inviting body, and, he suspected from her reactions, she was warm-blooded enough to respond to his interested glances.

What to do about it? was the question. Did jailers ever fraternize with their charges?

Thankfully his attention was diverted by a brace of wild turkeys waddling frantically from the thicket. A deer bounded into sight and, after a startled glance at Quinn, leapt toward a small grove of trees. A family of rabbits followed, stopped in their tracks and swerved to avoid Quinn. He wondered what had frightened them. The answer came in seconds when a large black bird flew into the air with a snake dangling from its bill.

This was the way he liked it: being outdoors and enjoying nature. Where he could forget he was in Sara's custody.

He was a drifter by choice and by habit. He'd been on his own since he'd run away at seventeen, and until last week, with a few exceptions, he'd been free, no ties to bind him, no one to answer to. He hadn't had a permanent home before and didn't need it now. As for material things, he'd never had much of those, either. Not that he cared. Everything he owned was in a single suitcase in his truck. It made it easier to keep moving on whenever he got itchy feet, and they were itching something fierce right now.

He glanced back at Sara. She'd driven another stake into the ground and was sitting back on her heels to rest. He'd never known anyone, man or woman, who worked as hard as she did. She deserved more than the bare existence she led, but she had to face the fact that it wasn't in his power to change things for her. Putting up fences sure didn't look as if it was going to make a difference in her financial security, no matter what she thought.

He was torn between his reluctant admiration for Sara Martin and her small family, and his instinctive desire to get out of Juniper before he was caught up in her problems. His frustration grew until he couldn't bear to think of it anymore.

When had this tiny blond tigress of a woman and two small children become important to him?

Sara gave up trying to tie her hair into a ponytail. It was too hot, anyway, she thought as she shook her hair to let the warm air blow through it. It wasn't only the air that was hot. Her body was on fire, too, and it wasn't from the ninety-plus-degree heat, either.

It was that damn hired hand of hers who was getting her stirred up. His aura of masculinity was driving her out of her mind, what little of it she had left after seeing him in brief, skintight shorts and listening to his sexual innuendoes.

Not that she was a prude, but ever since Steven had disappeared from her life, she'd kept her mind off the subject of sex. She'd made a choice between it and her role as caretaker to the twins. Until Quinn Tucker came along, the choice had been easy. Juniper's male population was every bit as sorry as she'd told him it was. Maybe, with a very few exceptions, worse. She didn't need any more problems on her hands. They were full enough already.

The fact that there were nineteen more days of having him around didn't help any, she thought as she counted off the next few feet and knelt down to place another marker. She would just have to try harder before she landed up as another woman passing through his life. If anyone got hurt, it would be her.

Sara straightened and stole a glimpse at Quinn. He was standing motionless, gazing off into the distance. Fading sunlight glinted through his ebony hair and across his suntanned face. His air of raw masculinity set off warning bells. She told herself it would be best not to be too attracted, too soft. But, in spite of all her best intentions not to get emotionally involved with him, she felt an overwhelming desire to rest her cheek against his chest, listen to his heart beat, to find out if it was beating as hard as hers.

She knew thoughts like these were dangerous. He was an unknown quantity. And a temporary one. Still, she had to give him credit; no matter what he'd done before she'd found him in jail, he'd been square with her.

She groaned. There was no way she wanted to be attracted to this man, but her hormones just wouldn't listen. She watched him slump over his shovel, run a hand through his hair; a sure sign of frustration if she ever saw one. Lord knew, the man had the right to be frustrated, even if he was his own worst enemy.

She knew she'd better keep her mind on business, but her body telegraphed the truth; Quinn was a man she was going to remember long after he'd gone out of her life. She folded her arms around her chest, willed herself not to care and turned her attention to priority one. Damn, where was that next boundary stone, anyway?

When she finally made her way back to Quinn, sweat beaded his forehead and he was leaning onto the posthole digger. "I think that's enough for today." She gestured at the partially fenced meadow. "We're making good progress. Thank you."

Quinn felt uneasy at her praise. She was getting friendly, and even though it was nice to have her thank him for a job he was doing only because he had to, he wasn't sure he was ready for "friendly."

"You're welcome," he mumbled.

As he started to shake the accumulation of soil from the posthole digger, it fell, catching him under his already-tender ribs before it landed across her feet. His muffled curse brought her to his side.

"Are you okay?" He was too breathless with pain to answer. "Here, let me see." He froze when she started to unbutton his shirt. Powerless to stop her, he let her do her Florence Nightingale thing. Her warm hands on his flesh as she gingerly prodded his ribs sent hot lines of desire coursing through him. By the time she reached the bruised ribs, her fragrance made his body stir, forget his pain. He wanted to pull her into his arms, bury his face in her lemon-scented hair. Kiss her moist lips. Satisfy the hunger that had been building up inside him for days.

He put his hands over hers and held them away from him. "Enough," he said gruffly, feeling ashamed for his wayward thoughts. Sara Martin was incredibly kind and gentle, probably more so than he deserved. He couldn't take advantage of her. "I'm okay, Ms. Martin. How about you?"

She stared up at him, unable to move her hand from under his. The warmth of his skin, the runaway heartbeat throbbing against her hand mesmerized her. She sensed a change in him, a change in her that frightened her. He was right. It was time to stop.

She dropped her hands and turned on her heel. "That's enough for today. I have to get back to start supper. Button up."

EVERY BUMP IN THE ROAD on the way back to the ranch threw them together. Her flesh was warm and soft, his grew warmer with each contact. When she shifted gears, the vintage truck swayed from side to side. It was all he could do to remain on his side of the seat.

He groaned. He didn't know which bothered him more, her womanly softness or the painful ache in his ribs. How else could he explain the physical attraction he felt for a woman who was his jailer? A woman who literally owned him? The very thought of being owned made his flesh crawl. He smothered a sigh of relief when the house came in sight.

A trickle of sweat was making its way down Quinn's back. His shirt was sticking to his aching body. "By the way, is it all right to take a hot shower and change into some more of those clothes upstairs? This shirt is beginning to get uncomfortable."

Her gaze was drawn to the broad chest outlined beneath his damp shirt. Somehow it seemed more muscular now that he'd been doing manual labor for a week. With a determined tilt to her chin and an odd smile tugging at her lips, she pointed to the stairs. "First room on the right. There's some men's clothing in the closet. Take your pick. You'll find soap and towels in the bathroom."

Whistling, Quinn headed for the upstairs shower. Sara's presence was everywhere in the single bathroom the family shared, from her robe and slippers to her toiletries on the counter. The scent of lemons hung heavily in the air. He used Sara's shampoo to wash his hair. Its tart lemon fragrance brought her image clearly to his closed eyes. His hands ached to cup her small, proud breasts, to taste her full lips against his own, to feel her curves pressed against him.

Damn! With Sara no longer acting as if he were an unwelcome guest, he was letting his imagination get out of hand. He turned on the cold water full blast and let it jolt him back to reality. After a week digging in the hard-packed earth, he was in no condition to do anything about his fantasy, even if she had been willing.

He wrapped a towel around his middle and wandered into the bedroom Sara had indicated. From the look of things, it had belonged to Amy McClintock and her husband, and she'd apparently kept it just as though he would return. His suits still hung in the closet, his shirts and underwear were in the dresser drawers. Even his comb and hairbrush sat neatly on top. His heart ached for the late Amy McClintock, a woman who'd loved her husband even though he'd left her and their children.

He sat in a rocking chair and drew on a pair of trousers that were too tight in the waist and too short in the legs. The shirt he found in a drawer didn't fit much better. Wondering what kind of man would leave his wife and two newborn children to fend for themselves, he gritted his teeth and clenched his hands. If the guy was only here, he'd show him what he thought of him.

Who was he to cast stones? His own mother and father had given up his custody to his grandmother before he was two. By the time his grandmother had died, they were gone, too. He'd been passed from relative to relative until he couldn't take it any longer and had finally run away. Bitter and resentful, he'd started down the path that had turned him into a rolling stone, looking for adventure, finding only trouble. Too bad he hadn't had an Aunt Sara in his life.

The smell of freshly brewed coffee drew him into the kitchen. Even in the fading light of the afternoon, the kitchen sparkled. Starched green-and-white checkered curtains hung at the windows. An old glass milk bottle filled with freshly picked roses sat in the middle of the kitchen table.

Sara was preparing chicken for dinner. Quinn paused in the doorway to admire the way she went about patting the bird dry, rubbing it with fresh garlic and dusting it with dried rosemary leaves before she put it in a roasting pan. Foil-wrapped sweet potatoes waited on the corner of the table. His mouth watered.

Intending to keep his emotional distance, he moved closer to her side, only to be done in by the scent of garlic mingled with the fragrance of her lemon shampoo. Strangely enough, the aroma was enough to make his body ache and his mind do tricks. As for Sara, from the wary glances she kept giving him, he was willing to bet she wasn't as unaware of him as she pretended to be.

They stood inches apart, but the look in her eyes kept him in his place. Maybe, he reasoned, it was because she still thought of him only as a criminal, not to be trusted. Damn! There were nineteen more days of this... He forced himself to be objective. She had a right to keep him at arm's length, since he hadn't come highly recommended. She might not know anything about him, but he was beginning to know a lot about her. Primarily, that she wasn't as coldhearted as she tried to be.

Driven by a need he didn't dare identify, he leaned close to her, inhaled her lemon scent and gently cupped her shoulder. She started, raised her head, lips parted. He fought the desire to taste those lips, drink in the taste of her. His eyes roamed freely over her tanned face, searching for and finding the name to describe this strong but vulnerable woman. "Sam," he murmured. The name escaped from his lips before he could catch himself.

"Sam?" Sara blinked. "What does that mean?"

"Sorry, the name just slipped out." He felt like a fool, but continued. "Calling you Ms. Martin is a bit old-fashioned, don't you think? Is it okay if I call you Sam?"

"I've never had a nickname before, but why Sam?"

"From your initials, Sara Ann Martin, but mostly because you're one tough lady."

For a moment she looked uncertain, but he guessed the look of admiration in his eyes satisfied her. "Yes, you may. I'll take it as a compliment, I think."

"A compliment was intended." Quinn was somehow pleased. He was glad to find she wasn't angry he'd gotten familiar with her. Giving her a nickname had been an impulse. Still, the name suited Sara and the triple role she played: mother, father and aunt. She was also a gentle and caring woman under her studied tough veneer.

"Sam, then," he agreed as he met her pleased expression. The name rolled off his tongue with an ease that surprised him. It was a name meant for this woman, and only this woman.

He wandered to the sink and poked around the small mound of salad greens dripping dry on the sink. As he reached for a carrot stick, he realized that the comforting kitchen activity brought back memories of his grandmother's kitchen and made him feel relaxed and easy. And Sara Martin was making him feel as if he belonged. No wonder he thought of her as sweet Sara Ann Martin. Sam.

Sara placed their dinner into the oven and wiped her hands. "Coffee?"

"Yes, thanks."

She moved past him to the stove where the coffee-pot perked. "Maybe we should drink it outside. It's kind of warm in here. You can take some of the cookies, if you like. Dinner won't be ready for an hour or so."

Chocolate chip cookies were his all-time favorite, and his ribs hurt enough to make him feel he owed himself a cookie or two.

He followed Sara to the table under the apple tree and settled down to enjoy the hot coffee and cookies. With the air gently stirring the leaves, it was cool under the tree. Sara's lemon scent filled his nostrils. Filtered sunlight cast glints of gold in her hair, so inviting that he was tempted to reach out and touch them to see if they were real gold. He glanced at her over the rim of his cup. There was a faraway look in her eyes and a soft smile on her face as she sipped her coffee. A faint pink tinged her cheeks. Curious, he wondered where her thoughts had gone.

"What are you thinking about, Sam?"

Sara bit her lip and gazed down into her cup. Butterflies danced in her stomach at the sound of his voice. If he only knew her wayward thoughts had been on that bit of damp hair that showed just above the top button on his shirt. To her chagrin, just being around his unconscious masculinity seemed to fascinate her. She tried to concentrate on his question.

"Sam?" The unexpected tenderness in Quinn's voice sent a wave of emotion through her. That's what nicknames were all about, she realized. People cared for you or they wouldn't bother to give you a nickname. Even though she knew he was only passing through her life, he behaved as if what she was thinking really mattered to him.

She'd heard the question, but her body obviously was hearing something else. She glanced up at him; her mouth went dry. He didn't need an open shirt to make her senses spin. The low timbre of his voice and the concern in his gaze threw her. As she met his questioning hazel eyes, she was shaken by her strong response to him. They hardly knew each other.

Still, Quinn acted as if he cared. It had been a long time since a man, or anyone for that matter, had asked her how she felt, or what she thought. He touched a part of her she'd firmly put behind her when Steven had walked out of her life. She'd put everything aside, dedicated herself to Amy and the children, but now she realized how much she'd missed.

Maybe it was the compassion she heard in his voice, or the wish for comfort that drew her, but Sara felt the need to share some of her thoughts with Quinn. But she'd have to be careful. He was a man passing through her life. In a few weeks he'd be gone.

"I was wondering if boarding horses is enough to make the ranch pay. I have to do something to take care of the children. Their social-security survivor's benefits aren't enough even now. What will it be like when they go to school?"

"Really? I wouldn't think that boarding horses was a subject that would have made your cheeks turn pink," he teased. He reached across the table to take her hand in his. "Sorry. Maybe I shouldn't be doing this."

He didn't take his hand away.

Neither did she.

Her eyes met his. "You've nothing to be sorry for."

"Thank you, Sam."

Sara felt herself blush again with pleasure when Quinn lightly ran his thumbs in circles around the back of her hand. When he said "thank you," there was a flash of fire in his eyes that made her feel like butter melting on hot toast.

There ought to be a law against a smile like his, she thought, a smile destined to drive any sensible thoughts right out of a woman's mind. She focused on his lips and wondered what they would have felt like on hers if he'd kissed her when they stood side by side in the kitchen. He had looked as if he wanted to. And, heaven help her, she wished he had.

She couldn't meet his eyes. His male scent stirred her in a way she didn't want to be stirred. The teasing look she'd seen in his eyes and his raised eyebrow challenged her in a way she didn't want to be challenged. She knew better than to tell him how she felt. It would never do to let him know that he'd gotten to her. Not if she intended to hold him to their bargain. And she had to.

She eased her hand away from his, took a deep breath and looked up at him. His hair was still damp around the edges from his shower; drops of water had flattened his shirt against his broad, muscular chest. His face was smooth and more tanned than when she'd first laid eyes on him. A week in the sun had done its work. He was beginning to look like a true outdoorsman. That air of masculinity he wore like a comfortable suit of clothing almost undid her good intentions. She didn't know what was the matter with her, but she wasn't going to stick around him to find out.

Sara drew in a quick breath and gulped the last of her coffee. "I really have to get back to our dinner." She pulled her hand away, glanced at his chest then turned on her heel and rushed to the kitchen door.

Since he knew dinner was already in the oven, Quinn was surprised at her abrupt departure. He was even more surprised when the screen door banged behind her. Making a mental reminder to fix the hinges on the door before he left, he rested his chin on his folded hands and thought about Sara's odd behavior. He didn't know what ailed the lady this time—after all, except for the top button, his shirt was securely fastened. He toyed with the button, fingered his shirt collar, gazed speculatively at the house, then broke into a satisfied male smile. There was something about his shirt that disturbed Sara. Whatever it was, he knew he'd found a way to soften her up. The devil in him urged him on. It was going to be a matter of time before Sara gave in and helped him buy his way out of here.

Chapter Four

He could hear bursts of childish exuberance and Sara's laughing voice. From the amount of noise coming from the kitchen, it sounded as if a whole ball team were in there having a free-for-all, but it had to be only Jase, and the normally quiet Katie, giggling and shrieking with pleasure. He paused to listen, and his thoughts turned back in time.

Nowhere, except in his grandmother's house, had there ever been such happy moments. At least not for him, the unwanted child. Smiling wistfully, Quinn downed the rest of his cold coffee and made his way back into the house to see what was going on.

He paused at the kitchen screen door, inspected its loose hinges and decided to fix them while he was thinking about it. It was a small repair, a matter of straightening the door and pounding in a few loose nails that hung by a thread. It wouldn't take a carpenter to fix it, although he'd done a bit of carpentry now and then. It would only take a moment of his time to repair it. He looked around him, spotted a rock big enough to do the job and hammered in the nails. Standing back and wryly inspecting the result, he made a mental note to get new nails and a decent hammer from Miguel, to come back and do the job properly. A simple job like this deserved being done right.

For that matter, he mused as he gazed around him, there were more than a few things that needed attention, including the worn wooden steps leading to the kitchen door. Not only did they creak when stepped on, they sagged to one side, a sure sign they were old and needed repair. Just like the house and the rest of the ranch. As soon as his ribs eased up on him, he'd take them on, one at a time, before he left. As long as he was still here, he amended, not really knowing why he should be assailed by doubts about leaving.

Maybe it was because he'd been too busy to find a way to get out of town without leaving his truck and his belongings behind him.

Or, maybe it was because he found those two kids and their aunt were like magnets, drawing him to them in a way he had yet to understand.

At any rate, he figured he had plenty of time to decide what to do. There was no hurry. Outside of a few days camping out in the mountains, he hadn't decided where his next stop would be, anyway.

Inside the house, he found Sara had set out a huge metal tub, the kind his grandmother must have used for doing laundry before washing machines made their appearance, and had filled it with water. Jase and Katie were having a water fight, and waves of water were splashing over the edge of the tub.

"Watch out, you're getting water all over me!" Sara laughed as she jumped out of the way. "I've already washed, it's you guys who need the bath after playing in the garden."

"We weren't playing in the garden, Aunt Sara." Jase managed to look offended. "We were working. Miguel said we're doing something very important."

"Indeed you are," Sara rejoined as she ruffled the boy's hair and kissed his forehead. "Very important. I don't know what I would do without the two of you taking care of that garden and supplying us with vegetables."

Mollified, Jase raised his face for a kiss and then turned his attention to his sister. "See, Katie? Aunt Sara really needs us."

Quinn cleared his throat when he saw the satisfaction in the kid's face and in his voice. It was obvious Sara's love blanketed the children and gave them a feeling of security. And for Jase, his confidence. No wonder the little guy was ready to take on the world. The last time anyone had done that for him was another lifetime ago.

"Hi, Mr. Tucker. We're taking a bath!"

"So I see." Quinn joined the group, crouched down, cocked his head and pretended to consider Jase's raised hand. "You're beginning to look like a wrinkled prune, fella."

Katie giggled. "I don't want to look like a prune, Aunt Sara. Can I get out now?"

Sara wrapped her in the large towel she was holding and wiped Katie's hair dry. "Mr. Tucker is only kidding. You'll never look like a prune, sweetheart. Princesses could never look like prunes."

"Me too, Aunt Sara. I'm not dirty anymore, look." Jase held up his hands for inspection. "Even my fingernails are real clean."

Sara helped him out of the tub and handed him another towel. "Upstairs, you two. Get some clean clothes on and come back down. Dinner will be ready soon."

"Lucky children," he said as he watched the laughing twins chase each other upstairs and disappear from sight. Unbidden, an unfamiliar emotion spread through him; a nostalgia for what had been his so briefly many years ago and never again. Until now, he hadn't realized how much he missed: a home of his own, loving parents, a sister, a brother. And now, it seemed, even a wife and children like Jase and Katie.

It wasn't like him to dwell on the past, he told himself. He just took one day at a time. He'd be wise to keep it that way.

"Lucky to have you," he added, turning back to look at Sara.

"Lucky me," Sara corrected as she mopped up the water on the floor. "They've made all the difference in my life. Without them, I could have drifted into a relationship with a man whose values were very different than my own and wound up just like my sister Amy." She sat back on her heels and gazed up at Quinn. "I was unhappy at first when my former fiancé left me, but as I came to know and love the twins, I knew I was blessed. I don't know what I'd do without them."

Quinn didn't know what to say. The fact that she was willing to share her feelings with him was touching, and a measure of how far they'd come since she'd bailed him out of jail. He was surprised to find the feeling was mutual. He no longer thought of her as his jailer, nor, surprisingly enough, of himself as a prisoner on parole.

"Here, let me," Quinn said as she started dragging the tub toward the door to empty the water. "I would have thought you'd use the bathroom upstairs. It's a lot more convenient."

"I usually do, but I wanted to give the kids a treat and let them play in the water while I finished dinner. I wouldn't dare leave them upstairs alone."

Quinn emptied the tub outside, set it to dry by the steps and came back into the kitchen. "Need any more help?"

"No, thanks. Everything's about done. I just have to make the pudding for dessert."

"Chocolate?"

"Of course. Don't you men like chocolate?"

"Sure, but how about you and Katie?"

"Katie likes what her brother likes, and I don't eat desserts."

"How can you resist chocolate pudding? It's one of my all-time favorites."

"The same way I can resist a lot of things," she answered with a smile that played at the corner of her lips.

"Don't resist. Take a risk. It adds a little spice to life."

They exchanged glances. He grinned and raised a questioning eyebrow. She blushed. Her look told him she understood exactly what he meant, and she wasn't buying.

Sara Ann Martin was a woman who invited teasing. Easily flustered, though she still gave as good as she got. He chalked up one more thing he liked about her.

"If it's pudding you're talking about, it's hardly worth the risk," she said firmly as she set a quart of milk on the table. "Now, if you want to be of help, hand me the pot from the cupboard over there."

He eyed her trim figure. Her jeans clung to her as if they had been painted on her skin, revealing womanly curves and angles. A white T-shirt decorated with elephants hugged each soft curve of her upper body. Yes indeed, he figured Sara Martin had a figure he might have dreamed of and was damn lucky to find. It was intriguing to see that she was utterly oblivious to the fact. She was a different sort of woman than the women he'd known; pragmatic, free of guile. Or was she?

Quinn dutifully got the pot down for her. "Now what?"

He watched while she measured out the milk, stirred in the mix and set the pot on the stove. "Stir this very slowly," she said as she handed him a wooden spoon, "while I get a bowl to put it in."

Back at the cupboard, she glanced over her shoulder at his clumsy efforts. "Slowly, or you'll have it all over the stove. Here, let me show you." She put her hand over his and stirred in a slow, circular motion. "See, slow hands work best."

With her hand on his and her breasts moving as she guided the stirring, it was all Quinn could do to keep his eyes on the wooden spoon. He knew that if he kept playing with fire, he was on the way to getting burned.

"Tell you what, I'll leave the cooking to you before I ruin it," he said uneasily. "I'd just as soon hang around the kitchen and talk, if you don't mind." He watched her as she took over the pudding. She stirred it slowly, her eyes on the stove, but she was doing a number on him just the same.

Sara didn't mind making the dessert by herself, even if it was difficult to keep her mind on the pudding with him watching her every move. Especially since she'd already sensed a difference in him, and even more so tonight.

"You've changed a lot, you know," she finally commented as she poured the hot mixture into the waiting bowl.

"Oh, in what way?"

"Well, for one thing, you're more relaxed, less angry. You haven't even mentioned getting out of here, lately. I even get the feeling you're comfortable here with us and, strange as it may have seemed a short time ago, even content to be on the Lazy M."

He stared at her, a look of surprise growing on his face. She realized he'd been unaware of the change in himself. He finally shrugged. "I guess I am. For now, anyway."

"Good." *For both of us,* she thought as she set the bowl in the ancient refrigerator.

"Sam?" He was contemplating the pudding-covered spoon he'd taken from the pot, watching her, his eyes tempting her. "Want a taste?"

"No, thanks." She picked up the pot and reached for the spoon. "Here, let me wash up."

"Maybe it's time for you to try the 'bad' side of life." He held the spoon away from her. Her hand felt like soft velvet, sending a thrill down his spine. Her eyes softened. "Well, maybe just a taste," she said as he held the spoon to her lips.

She took a taste, telling herself it was the only way to get rid of him, knowing all along she was fooling herself. Part of her wanted to take the risk he was offering, although she wasn't quite certain just what that risk was.

He was watching her, his eyes sparkling, inviting her. She sensed he was asking for something, something she couldn't give. Or wouldn't give, even if she could. Not now, not on demand. That's what was bothering her. He was always making innuendoes that provoked an unbidden response, though she didn't think he knew how he was getting to her. But if she gave in to those responses, she'd have to find a means of escape, no matter how tempted she was. Before she got hurt.

"Time for dinner." Keeping her face averted from him, she busied herself taking salad and butter out of the refrigerator. Now that he was cleaned up and his temper wasn't showing, the man was indecently attractive. She was having a hard time not revealing just how attractive she thought he was. She'd already admitted how different a man he'd become. It was in the gentle way he responded to the children, his growing appreciation of her small family and, yes, even his not-too-subtle interest in her.

The stirring of physical desire was troubling. Only a fool would fall into his arms, she thought as she called the children to the table. She was afraid the next few weeks wouldn't pass fast enough to suit her.

Dinner was a noisy affair, the children in high humor, Sara beaming, even Miguel smiling and making jokes throughout the meal. Quinn gazed around him and was surprised to find he *was* content. The feeling was new to him, since most of his days had been spent giving in to the urge to move on. He hadn't been able to stay in one place for more than a month or two for longer than he cared to remember. What surprised him most of all was the realization of how much the kids and Sara had gotten to him. Sara most of all.

He wasn't accustomed to introspection. Examining his thoughts left him uneasy, even blue. But these few days with Sara forced him to think of who he was, where he was going, what he was making of his life. And finding no ready answers. He had a lot of thinking to do.

HE WAS STILL WIDE AWAKE when dawn broke and the rooster crowed. He'd spent the night thinking about Sara and the children, especially Sara. She was a very special person, caring for everyone and putting her own needs last. She'd said that she was happy just being Aunt Sara, but he knew better. She was a woman capable of great depths and strong passions, no matter what she said. Now that he'd gotten to know her a little, he wanted to know more about her. What her thoughts were; her hopes, her fears, her dreams. She was a mixture of all the good qualities it took to make a good, decent human being. There weren't many of her kind around. He hadn't given her the nickname of Sam for nothing.

He tried to swing out of bed without waking Miguel, but the accident with the posthole digger had taken its toll. His ribs were aching something fierce. He sank back in bed, cursing the bad luck that continued to plague him. Until he remembered yesterday, and Sara's comments about the welcome change in him. Maybe his luck wasn't all bad, after all.

Cautiously he rose and pulled on his jeans. Grabbing his shirt, he made his way to the tiny bathroom.

His reflection in the mirror hanging over the basin made him grimace. No matter how badly he needed a shave, he couldn't raise his right arm for more than a few seconds before pain shot through his ribs. It was going to take more than his strong will to get him through the day.

He turned away as Miguel stirred. He was in no mood to exchange pleasantries with the old man, as nice as he was. He needed help more than conversation. He had a hard day's work ahead of him. Maybe Sara had aspirins in the house, or something stronger. Shirt over his shoulders, he made his way to the house.

She was in the kitchen baking biscuits and frying ham. Eggs waited on the counter. The table was set for breakfast. Coffee perked on the stove.

"Don't you ever sleep in?" Quinn asked.

"Not when there's work to be..." Her voice trailed off when she noticed he was hunched over. "Your ribs bothering you?"

"Yeah. I was hoping you had some aspirins."

"Wait a minute, I'll be right back."

He heard her footsteps climbing the stairs. She was back sooner than he'd expected, a bottle in one hand, a small white tube of medication in the other. She filled a glass with water and handed him two aspirins. "Sit down and take off your shirt. I have something here that will relieve some of the pain."

The odor coming from the ointment in the tube wasn't much better than the horse liniment Miguel had offered him. He wrinkled his nose in disgust. "Good lord, what's that?"

"Ointment made from the oil of eucalyptus leaves. I know it smells awful, but it'll soothe your muscles. I guarantee it. Here, let me help you."

She squeezed a glob of white ointment on one hand, leaned over him and gently spread it on his ribs. He held his breath. Luckily the strong odor seemed to disappear as Sara's freshly washed hair brushed his chin. The scent of her shampoo put his pain in second place.

"Stand up so I can reach you easier."

Quinn stood up cautiously and looked down at her bent head. Her tenderness as she massaged the ointment into his flesh overwhelmed him. A lump rose in his throat when he remembered the dozens of bruises he'd suffered and the lack of concern offered him.

He touched her hair, let the silken strands run through his fingers while she worked away at his ribs. When her hand stopped in mid-motion and she looked up at him, he bent and did what he'd been longing to do from the first time he'd laid eyes on her; he kissed her, gently at first, then again with an urgency that surprised him and seemed to surprise her as well. He lifted her against him and kissed her again. This time, his lips searched for and demanded a response.

Sara raised her arms to encircle his neck, closed her eyes and gave in to the fantasy that had kept her awake last night. A throbbing had begun in her middle and spread upward, causing her breasts to feel heavier, the tips to harden as she envisioned him kissing her lips, her breasts. She'd fantasized pressing closer to him and running her fingers through the ebony curls on his chest that had drawn her imagination from the first day in the Juniper jailhouse. In that midnight scenario, the soft locks of hair had curled around her fingers, caressing her as surely as Quinn's lips had caressed her breasts.

It had been a shameless dream. Where it was going to lead her, she didn't know. And, during the long night, she hadn't cared. Just as she didn't care now.

"Sorry," he said when he finally let her go.

She ran her hand across her eyes and licked her lips. "Good heavens, what was that all about?"

"Just what it felt like," he responded, running his finger over her bruised lips. "I'm not apologizing for kissing you, if that's what you think. But I am sorry if I hurt you."

"No. No..." She hesitated, lips trembling. "But the children will be down soon, and I think we should end this now."

"For now," he echoed. His eyes held a promise. She looked away.

In broad daylight, things looked different than they had during the long night. She didn't know how to handle that promise. "Breakfast is ready. I'll be right back. I forgot something in the pantry."

He followed her into the pantry and found her standing on her toes trying to reach a jar of jam. Closing his mind to the moments they'd just shared, he reached over her head. "This what you wanted, Sam?"

Fighting warring emotions, Sara turned to face him. His eyes still gleamed with interest and she doubted that it was the jar of jam that was the subject of his scrutiny. Every nerve in her body responded to him as she reached for the jar and hugged it to her chest. "Yes. Thanks."

Quinn's gaze followed the path of the jar. Sara hurriedly lowered her hands. "Is there something you wanted?"

"I was wondering if it would be all right with you if I moved into the spare bedroom in the house."

"What?"

"I asked if I could move into the house."

For a fleeting moment, she thought about what it would be like to have him in the same house with her. Sleeping in a bedroom across the hall, sharing her bathroom. Seeing him at breakfast in his half-opened shirt. Letting the scent of his shaving lotion fill her mornings. She wavered, knowing in her heart he wouldn't remain across the hall for long.

She was too aware of the way his eyes followed her, and her own turbulent response to him. Besides, she was more than afraid he was using her response to his kisses to soften her up. She hesitated, drew a deep breath and deliberately thrust desire behind her.

"I don't think so. It's not that I don't want you to use the room," Sara hurried to add before his magic appeal robbed her of any common sense she had left.

"It's just that people would talk if word got out that you were staying in the same house with me."

"To hell with what people would think!" The look of shock on her face sobered him. "Sorry, but I never expected you to say that after..." He gestured toward the kitchen.

Sara pushed her way past him. "That's precisely the point! What makes you think because we shared a few kisses you're home free? That you can move into the house and take over? You have an inflated idea of your own charms."

"That's a low blow." The color faded from his face. He shrugged his shoulders. "But, what the hell, who am I to expect life to be a rose garden? It hasn't been one before. Maybe I expected too much."

"Look here, a man who gets himself arrested and goes to jail isn't the kind of person any sane woman wants around if she's worried about her reputation." She met his angry gaze defiantly.

"You act as if I'm an ax murderer! I'm only guilty of resisting arrest by an ignorant sheriff."

"That was this time. From what the sheriff told me, you had a lot more serious problems before you got to Juniper. Heaven only knows what they were. But it doesn't make any difference. I have Jase and Katie to consider."

Quinn's voice grew tight with anger. "Oh, so now I'm not fit to be around children?"

"You have to put a lid on your quick temper, Quinn Tucker. I think you had better stay in the lean-to with Miguel until you do."

"You're saying you don't feel safe with me around?" Quinn's expression turned to ice. "Never mind my asking for the room. I wouldn't live in this house with you if you begged me to. And what's more," he said, as he stalked after Sara into the kitchen with deliberately heavy steps, "I'm going to get out of here as fast as I can. Eighteen more days. Right?" Sara nodded. "Then, Ms. Martin, you won't have to be afraid of me or what you think I might do."

Chapter Five

"Be careful with that rail, Mr. Tucker! At the rate you're going, you're going to have more than a few bruised ribs. And this time, you'll get no help or sympathy from me." Sara glared at Quinn, who was struggling with his end of the split rail.

"Yes, ma'am. Sorry, ma'am. Anything else you don't like about the way I'm doing my job?" he responded through clenched teeth, returning her glare as if daring her to push him too far.

"I'll be the first to let you know," Sara snapped, more than half aware that her exchange of heated words was a childish way to get even with him for losing his temper and walking out on her. Their newfound relationship had deteriorated into a "speak when spoken to" basis. Lord knew, they'd found little enough to talk about.

Mealtimes were the worst. Their silence seemed to puzzle the twins and Miguel. Every time she looked up from her plate or passed a dish of food, she saw three pairs of questioning eyes. And in Jase's, a certain sadness. She felt badly about Jase. He'd been so taken with Quinn. And Quinn with him.

If only she had been able to convince herself he hadn't been using his sensuality on her to get what he wanted.

She waited until he had his end of the rail in place and handed him a hammer. "Here, use this and set it in place a little more."

"Yes, ma'am." He swung the hammer so hard she saw pain shoot across his face. "Damn!"

"That ought to teach you to curb your temper! I would have thought you'd have learned by now you're your own worst enemy. Well, let me tell you, Mr. Tucker, I don't have to stay and listen to you sound off, either. If you can't be more civilized than that, you're on your own from now on."

"Fine with me, lady. I was doing okay on my own until I made the mistake of taking a road leading to this paradise called Juniper."

"You could have fooled me, Mr. Tucker. After all, I did find you in jail."

UNRELENTING NOONDAY HEAT beat down on Quinn as he struggled to lift a split rail into place. The granddaddy of all headaches pounded through his head and across his eyes. Perspiration ran down his back. Heat waves undulated, distorting the distant mountains. Blinded by brilliant rays of sunshine that bounced off the chrome trim of the pickup truck, he shaded his eyes with a shaking hand. As he struggled with the fence rail, he cursed the sheriff, the judge and the circumstances that had brought him here.

Sara didn't know it, but his temper had actually cooled in the three days since his quarrel with her about moving into the house. The argument they'd just had was all show on his part. His pride wouldn't let him be the first to apologize for the misunderstanding, and the result was that he was still bunking with Miguel. Too bad it was only his temper that had cooled, he thought wryly as the rail settled into the notched pole with a soft thud. The rest of him was burning up.

He wiped his forehead with his leather-clad hand. He'd gratefully accepted the worn gloves Miguel had insisted he wear. Too bad he hadn't thought to ask for a hat to shield him from the sun.

Glancing around to make certain Sara wasn't close enough to see what he was doing, he unbuttoned his shirt to let the air dry his damp skin. His chest felt tight and hot enough to fry that proverbial egg he'd heard so much about. He reached for the thermos of water Sara had urged on him. There was only a little liquid left. When he drained it dry, his mouth still felt as though it were coated with dust.

He wiped his damp forehead and tried to think of something cold. Iced coffee. Yeah, iced coffee would have tasted real good about now. It was the last coherent thought he had before the earth tilted up and smacked him in the face.

FROM WHERE SHE WAS driving a boundary stake into the hard ground, Sara glanced at her watch. It was almost one o'clock and time to break for lunch. She took off her hat, shook out her hair and squinted up at the sky. Cloudless, the clear turquoise atmosphere shimmered in the heat. Even here in the foothills of northern San Diego County the temperatures hovered in the nineties. Maybe she and Quinn should call it a day, she thought as she searched for the sight of him.

If he only knew that she couldn't stand being around him because of her attraction for him—not because she was angry. If she was angry with anyone, it was herself. Angry for "buying" him in the first place, angry for wanting to be held in his arms, angry for wanting more of his kisses.

She toyed with the idea of returning him to jail where she'd be removed from temptation. But the thought of what the sheriff would do to him stopped her. Remembering Quinn's numerous bruises, she knew, whatever else he was guilty of, he didn't deserve being sent back to Cable's mercies.

She wandered back to where she'd last seen him. Her heart skipped a beat when she saw him lying in a heap beside the fence. She sprinted across the space that separated them and dropped to her knees.

"Quinn?"

She shook his shoulder. He was still, too still. She touched his forehead—he was burning up! She needed water. The thermos lying beside Quinn was empty.

Frantically she raced to the truck, grabbed the thermos of lemonade she'd packed for their lunch and ran back to Quinn's side. Pulling Quinn's shirt aside, she dipped a corner into the cool drink, wiped his lips and splashed some of the lemonade on his forehead and chest.

"Quinn! Can you hear me?"

He stirred for a second, only a second, before he fell unconscious again.

Sara was frightened and frustrated at her own helplessness. "Quinn, can you hear me? I can't lift you by myself. I've got to go for help. Don't move. I'll be right back," she cautioned over her shoulder as she ran to the truck, jumped in and sped away.

Someone was telling him not to move. It was fine with him. Lemonade, it was raining lemonade, Quinn thought dimly as he licked his lips. Right on! The Big Guy knew just what Quinn needed. He tried to open one eye. A red mist covered the sky. Pink lemonade? he wondered as he sank back into a cool, black darkness.

WHEN SHE FINALLY RETURNED with help, Quinn was still completely out and limp as a rag doll. He weighed too much for them to handle him gently. Sara prayed hard as she, Miguel and the twins wrestled Quinn into the truck bed. Handing the twins folded wet towels, she instructed Katie to hold one to Quinn's forehead and Jase to wipe his lips with another. Her heart sank when the cool towels didn't revive him. "What do you think is the matter with him, Miguel?"

"I think Señor Quinn has the stroke of the sun, Miss Sara."

"Sunstroke? Of course! Good heavens, it's all my fault. I should have known he's not used to working in the sun. I should have insisted that he wear one of your hats. Do you think he'll be okay?"

Quinn moaned and muttered so softly Sara couldn't understand what he was saying.

"Oh no, now he's delirious!"

"Do not worry, Miss Sara." Miguel tried to shade Quinn's face with his own hat. "He will be better soon."

Sara checked Quinn's forehead and frowned at the heat she felt there. "Maybe I should call a doctor."

Miguel shrugged and crossed himself. "It is in God's hands, Miss Sara."

Miguel's gesture, and the pious prayer he uttered, sent a wave of pure terror through Sara. She told the twins to continue to hold a damp towel to Quinn's head, climbed into the cab, floored the gas pedal all the way back to the house and skidded to a halt by the front door.

"We'll put him in the parlor for now so I can take care of him."

"I don't know, Miss Sara," Miguel said doubtfully. "Mr. Quinn, he is a big man and the parlor so far."

"We can't leave him here in the truck. Move him to the edge and we'll do the best we can."

Miguel held Quinn's head and shoulders, Sara supported his waist and the two children each took hold of one of Quinn's legs. Together, they carried him into the cool, dark room and lowered him onto the couch.

He smelled of perspiration and lemonade and was out like a burned-out light. Trying hard not to dwell on Quinn's damp chest, Sara took off his shirt. The broad, muscular chest that had plagued her from the first moment she glimpsed it under his unbuttoned shirt plagued her still. Soft black curls wound themselves around her fingers as she carefully dried him off with a clean towel. Snatching her fingers away, she flushed as she remembered her reaction the first time she glimpsed a curl showing above his undershirt neckline. Every time the curls were exposed, she felt like a teenager stricken at her first sight of a nude male chest.

There had to be something wrong with her to think of something so sensuous at a time like this.

She felt the side of Quinn's neck for his pulse. It was beating wildly, almost as wildly as her own. He groaned and muttered a disjointed sentence. She had to hurry. She turned her attention to his belt and stopped her hand in midair; she couldn't handle the rest.

"Miguel, will you loosen his belt while I get a basin of water and some more towels?" Sara laid a wet towel over Quinn's chest.

"Sí." Casting a sympathetic eye at Sara, Miguel nodded and bent to wrestle with the belt buckle.

"Katie, you and Jase go get some clean sheets from the closet for Miguel."

"Is Mr. Tucker going to be all right?" Jase edged to the couch for a closer look. "I really like him, Aunt Sara. I don't want anything to happen to him."

"He's going to be fine, sweetheart, just as soon as we make him comfortable. Now, hurry."

Shivering with excitement, the twins ran from the room while their aunt headed for the kitchen.

When Sara returned, Quinn was modestly covered with a cool cotton sheet and still unconscious. She drew aside the sheet across his chest and prepared to bathe him with tepid water. Praying hard that cooling him down would bring him out of his stupor, she soaked a towel, wrung it out and started sponging his still-heated chest.

She'd gotten past his forehead and was gently dabbing his lips when she heard a faint murmur. Relieved to have him conscious again, Sara leaned forward to hear what Quinn was saying. "Water? Do you want water?"

He wrinkled his forehead, ran his tongue across his parched lips and shook his head.

"What does Mr. Quinn want, Miss Sara?" Miguel hovered at her side, a worried look on his face.

"I must be mistaken. It sounded as if he said pink lemonade, but I'm certain he meant water." She felt

Quinn's forehead again. "The man is delirious. Maybe I should call a doctor!"

"More," Quinn whispered.

Just then Jase wandered back into the room with Katie trailing after him and came over to the couch to listen to Quinn's muttering. "He wants some lemonade, Aunt Sara." Katie nodded solemnly.

"How do you know that?"

"Because that's what we want when we're thirsty, don't we, Katie?"

Sara studied Quinn. He was tossing on the couch, reaching out his hand. "Well," she said doubtfully, "if that'll make him better, it's worth a try. There's a pitcher of lemonade in the fridge. Jase, do you think you can pour some into a glass?"

"Sure I can, Aunt Sara!" Jase dashed for the kitchen and soon returned with a dripping glass of lemonade.

Together, Miguel and Sara helped Quinn sip the drink, laid him back on the couch and covered him with the sheet. "Let him rest a bit. He doesn't look too good. I think I will call the doctor."

Moments later, Sara was back, reading from penciled notes she'd taken over the telephone. "Dizziness, headaches, sweating, faintness, clammy to the touch. Dr. Watkins says Quinn's suffering from a bad case of heat exposure. Thank goodness it's not sunstroke."

"What do we do now, Miss Sara?"

"First, I have to make some salt water for Quinn to sip."

"Salt water?" Katie shook her head. "I think Mr. Tucker would rather have lemonade."

"Dr. Watkins suggested saltwater tablets, but I don't think there's any around. Not that Quinn could swallow them, anyway. Salt water will have to do," Sara said firmly. "And then, we'll take him upstairs and put him to bed."

The twins gazed wide-eyed at Quinn's unconscious figure then back at their aunt. "Upstairs, Aunt Sara?"

"Upstairs. We got him into the house, and we'll just have to get him up there and into bed." Sara had her doubts whether she was doing the wisest thing by moving Quinn to the upstairs bedroom, but the poor man was obviously very sick. She felt responsible. "He'll be more comfortable there and I can keep an ear out for him during the night."

Miguel smiled.

The twins grinned.

Sara sighed. Quinn had gotten himself invited into the house after all. It was the hard way to success but he was here, inside—and she'd done it herself.

SOMETIME in the early-morning hours, Sara heard sounds coming from Quinn's room. She shot out of bed and rushed to the room across the hall in time to see him struggling to get out of bed.

"What do you think you're doing?" She urged him back on the pillows. "You're too weak to get out of bed by yourself."

Quinn cast a bleary eye at Sara. Even in his weakened state, he could see she was a sexy dish in an oversize T-shirt that clung to her curves in a way to make a man weak, if he wasn't already at death's door. Her hair was an unruly bundle of burnished gold and hung down her back. Long, slender bare legs ended in charming pink toes. Interesting, he thought vaguely, but he had something more urgent to do right now than inspect the intriguing little lady.

"Sam, if you don't let me get to the bathroom, we're both going to be sorry."

"Oh!" She felt wave after wave of heat suffuse her body. How stupid can one gal get, she thought as she fought her embarrassment. "Right!"

She backed away from the bed. Considering the amount of liquid she'd been pouring down his throat, Quinn must be mighty uncomfortable. "Can you manage by yourself?"

"I've been doing all right in that department ever since I was about two years old."

"You're suffering from heat exposure, you big lug. You don't know how sick you've been. I only asked because I wouldn't want to have to pick you up off the floor."

"Okay, help me if you feel you must, but you're not going to stay inside with me!"

"I wouldn't dream of it."

Quinn threw a bare leg over the edge of the bed before he realized he was nude beneath the sheets; not even his Jockey shorts had been left to him. Images of Sara wrestling the clothes off his back brought a cautious question to his lips. "Who undressed me? You?"

"The heat must have unhinged your mind. I wouldn't dream of it. Miguel and Jase did the honors. Now get up before you have an accident."

He bit back the laugh that shook him. "Sam, unless you want to see me in my birthday suit..."

Sara turned her back.

A muffled sound of impatience turned her around, she swallowed the desire to laugh. He'd wrapped himself togalike in the sheet and was tripping on its loose ends. Straight-faced, she offered him her arm and supported him across the hall to the bathroom.

"Call me when you're ready."

He shot her a wicked grin. "If I was in better shape—"

"Don't even think about it!"

"Yes, ma'am."

A few minutes later, Sara heard a thud and a muted curse coming from the bathroom. Holding her breath, she called, "Are you decent? I'm coming in!"

She cautiously opened the door to see Quinn sitting on the floor in a tangle of sheets, hands raised in surrender. "I guess I wasn't in as good a shape as I thought I was. Help me back to bed, will you?"

"Please."

"Please. You're sure hard on a guy when he can't fight back, Sam. Wait until I feel better and I'll take you on."

"When you feel better, you're going back to the lean-to, Mr. Tucker."

Kneeling down until she was at his level, she helped him to his knees and tried to adjust the sheet around him. They were so close, his body heat made her own temperature rise. The cold linoleum floor finally forced her to her feet. As she rose, his lips were inches away from her ear. A lemonade-laced breath surrounded her when he whispered, "You look great in that shirt, Sam."

Suddenly Sara was conscious of the worn T-shirt she slept in. She crossed her arms over her chest. "Is that all you can think of in a crisis?"

"Thank goodness for the crisis," Quinn said, with a leer.

"That's enough! Hold on to my arm while I get you back to bed, or I'll let you spend the day right here."

She was rewarded by a grin and Quinn's outstretched hand. Smothering a smile, she helped him to the bed and fluffed up the pillows behind his head. "You could use a dose of humility, not to mention a showing of gratitude."

"Did I forget to say thank you? Sorry." He sank back against the feather pillows, and closed his eyes. "Excuse me, I have to wait until the room stops spinning and those drums stop beating before I can thank you properly. By the way, Sam, did you know it rained pink lemonade today?"

"Only in your dreams." She felt his forehead. He was warm, but cooler than before. "You were having hallucinations, Mr. Tucker."

"Really? Too bad, I sure could use some pink lemonade right now."

"First, sip some more of this." She held a glass of liquid to his lips.

"My God!" He gagged on the liquid. "Are you trying to poison me? What is that?"

"Salt water. Dr. Watkins said it will help."

"That's cruel and inhuman punishment, and a heck of a way to get even with me, Sam." He pushed the glass away. "I'd much rather have pink lemonade."

"Sorry, we're all out of pink. If you behave yourself I'll bring you some lemonade later." When he managed to look crestfallen, Sara relented. "Actually, you need to drink as much liquid as you can. I suppose lemonade will do just as well." She backed out of the room with as much dignity as she could muster. "I'll be back soon."

Quinn tried to pull his thoughts together. For an independent, freedom-loving guy, he wasn't doing too well. Too weak to fight, his life had taken a strange turn—marching to the tune of a drummer over whom he had no control.

Judging from the short time he'd known her, Sara was the kind of woman he'd done his best to avoid: a nest builder who needed a man who would be happy

to come home to her every night. A man who had a
safe and secure nine-to-five job. The eternal earth
woman, a good Samaritan, sensitive and loving. Nice
to know, but one who played for keeps.

As for him, he was the first to admit he was the
restless type, needed his space. The only women he'd
ever been involved with were the kind who posed no
threat to his freedom. When he'd kissed them goodbye, there had been no tears or recriminations. He'd
never been bored and, he hoped, he'd never been bor-
ing.

To him, life was a quest, full of adventures. At
thirty, he figured he still had time to pursue a whole
list of them. He and Sara Ann Martin were totally
unalike.

So why did she make him feel hungry?

Hungry for the smile that curved on her lush lips,
for the eager look that came into her coffee-colored
eyes when she thought he wasn't looking. For the
warm, full breasts that brushed against him when she
helped him back to bed and yes, even for the quick,
sharp words of reproof she kept throwing his way.

Dimly, he knew it had something to do with his
chest. If only he could figure out why his shirts seemed
to bother Sam so much, he thought as he drifted off
to sleep.

SHOWERED AND DRESSED in fresh clothing, Sara
quietly made her way downstairs. She'd hidden her

T-shirt in the laundry basket, determined not to wear it again until Quinn was long gone from the Lazy M.

The name suited the ranch and its original owner, her father, Dan Martin, she thought as she tiptoed past the twins' room. Lazy. She remembered when he christened the ranch. No use working too hard, or improving it too much, he'd said. It was going to be a weekend retreat, a place to relax and play. No one had figured the day would come when the ranch would have to provide a livelihood for the family he and Mom had left behind. It was why she'd gone to Los Angeles to work, leaving her sister and her sister's new husband, Richard McClintock, behind. The ranch had been good for little then, and it looked as if it wasn't going to be good for much now.

If she'd only known what the next five years would bring, she would have been better prepared financially to care for her sister and her children. Her sister's illness had taken most of the money she did have, and it had been touch and go ever since.

Dawn was breaking as she entered the kitchen. It was going to be another scorcher. The children were still asleep and probably Miguel, too. Just as well, she thought as she quietly left the house to gather lemons to make more lemonade. It looked as if she was going to have her hands full with Quinn.

Spike, the mule, complained behind his fence when she started back. She was about to throw him some hay when Miguel appeared from the lean-to.

"Buenos días, Miss Sara. You are up early. Mr. Quinn is okay, yes?"

"It was too hot for me to stay in bed. Quinn's been up and back to sleep again. Just as well. He doesn't look too good."

"You need help?"

"Thanks, I'll manage. Just take care of Spike, here, and try to keep him quiet." She waved and started for the house. "I'll call if I need you."

Sara sliced and squeezed lemons into a large pitcher. Too bad it wasn't raining pink lemonade the way Quinn believed. It would have saved her a lot of work. All she had was the good old yellow garden variety of lemons. They would have to do, she thought until she remembered the jars of cherries she'd put up last spring. If Quinn wanted pink lemonade, pink lemonade he would have. She smiled as she poured some of the red liquid into the pitcher.

The strong, angry man she'd bailed out of jail had become a man she hadn't bargained for. A tease, a charmer, and truly humorous, to boot. Dependable, hardworking, and good with Katie and Jase. Miguel treated him with respect and deferred to Quinn's judgment. She didn't know what to make of the extraordinary man she'd found.

She set a pot of coffee to perk, knowing she was going to need it to see her through a rough day taking care of the ranch, the twins, and now, Quinn.

He was different from the men she'd known. In the short time he'd been at the ranch, he'd proved to be a man she could trust, even if he did have a dubious past. She hadn't counted on finding someone like him, not after her breakup with Steven. And certainly not with the twins as a daily reminder of her sister's unhappy experience with Richard McClintock.

She'd let Quinn into her life without realizing it and had come to care for him too much. She didn't want that, couldn't afford it, wouldn't allow it. Not when she knew he would leave as soon as his sentence was over. She didn't need another Steven in her life—not even on a temporary basis.

Absently she took several cookies out of the cookie jar and noted that the cookie level was low. Heat or no heat, she'd have to bake in the next day or so.

It wasn't going to be easy, she thought as she poured herself a cup of strong, black coffee. She felt as though Quinn's sentence had become hers, that their lives had somehow become interwoven. Instead of treating him like a hired hand, he was sleeping like a king upstairs in a feather bed and she was making him pink lemonade, of all things! She had only herself to blame.

Daylight was peeking through the open window in Quinn's room when she carried the pitcher upstairs. "Here you go, pink lemonade, no ice. I didn't think..." Her voice trailed away when she realized Quinn had fallen asleep. Beads of perspiration had broken out on his forehead; his complexion had faded from a bright pink to a pale white. It was obvious that he was very weak and a long way from being able to get out of bed.

She put the pitcher of lemonade on the nightstand. He could have his drink when he awakened. Insisting that he move to the lean-to was now out of the question.

"Aunt Sara?"

Jase and Katie were standing in the doorway. He had his favorite stuffed dog, Shelby, under his arm. She held a teddy bear to her chest.

"Yes, sweethearts?"

"The animals are hungry, Aunt Sara. Can they have breakfast?"

"Soon." Sara handed two cookies to the twins. "See if they'll settle for these for now. Go back to bed, it's very early. I'll have breakfast going before long."

Pretending to feed the animals, the twins backed out of the door and raced down the hall to their room.

Sara put a cookie beside the pitcher and sat down in the rocking chair. Quinn liked chocolate chip cookies, too.

Silently studying him as he lay sleeping, she acknowledged how much the man intrigued her, and had from the first time their eyes had met through the iron bars of the jail. When he awakened, she was going to make it her business to find out more about him. It was only fair. After all, he knew a great deal about her. Not that it really mattered, she had nothing to hide, but there was something about Quinn that told her maybe *he* did.

Her fingers itched to move the coal black hair away from his eyes, to soothe the frown from his forehead as she sometimes did with small Jase. When Quinn muttered in his sleep and tossed the sheet off his chest, she was forcibly reminded he was no four-year-old boy. With his broad shoulders, hard biceps and muscled chest that tapered to a lean waist, he was a virile specimen of a man. He was also a man who would walk out of her life as easily as he had walked into it.

She sighed heavily and rose to cover him. Life was strange, she thought as she settled herself in the rocker again. None of her carefully laid plans had come true. Instead of being a wife with a husband to share her life, she was alone with more responsibilities than she'd ever dreamed of. She was a mother to twins without ever having borne a child, a rancher without the means to make the ranch pay, and a woman with an uncertain future. She was tired, oh so tired, and the padded rocking chair so comfortable.

She leaned back, closed her eyes and let herself sink into a pleasant dream.

Chapter Six

Quinn slowly awakened and promptly wished he hadn't. His head felt as heavy as a bowling ball, his mouth as dry as if he'd been chewing dust. What he needed was a drink of pink lemonade or a drink of water, real water, no matter what the doctor had recommended. He'd be damned if he'd settle for salt water again.

He ran his hand over his aching eyes and gazed around the dimly lighted room. His body was beginning to telegraph a need he didn't think he could handle any better than he had the last time, but the thought of landing on the cold bathroom floor again was more than he could bear. No better was the prospect of having to have Sara help him back to bed. Not after the way they'd parted.

When *had* they been together out in the south pasture working on the fence? Yesterday? Today? His head pounded a Souza march. He couldn't remember. He did remember she'd been angry with him, glaring over her shoulder as she walked away. If looks could have killed, he'd be a dead man by now. He wasn't sure if she'd gotten over her anger, but he wasn't going to put himself at her mercy and find out.

It was a question of mind over matter, he decided. He'd wait until he felt stronger and make the trip to the bathroom on his own.

He glanced over at the nightstand and saw a pitcher of pink lemonade and an empty glass. Sighing his relief, he was happy to see that there was a lemonade angel after all.

A cookie rested next to the pitcher. His angel had even remembered his weakness for chocolate chip cookies. He tried to sit up, fell back and contemplated the logistics of pouring himself a glass of lemonade.

Pink lemonade.

Nothing was going to stop him.

He inched toward the edge of the bed and, taking a pillow with him, rolled to his left side. Stuffing the pillow under the shoulder that rested on the mattress, he propped himself against it and reached for the glass. So far, so good, he thought with satisfaction as he took the glass in his left hand. The effort drained what little strength he had left. Resting for a moment, he mulled over his next move. The pitcher of pink lemonade was the gold ring. He reached for it.

A muffled groan and the clink of glass against glass awakened Sara. She jumped to her feet in time to see Quinn struggling to pour himself a glass of lemonade from the dripping pitcher and lunged to catch it before it fell.

"You should have called me!" she scolded. "You could have poured the whole pitcherful over you!"

"That's not such a bad idea. I remember how good it felt when it rained pink lemonade." Quinn's features took on a dreamy look. "Tasted good, too."

"Rained pink lemonade," Sara scoffed, as she replaced the pitcher on the nightstand. "You were having hallucinations."

"No way. It rained pink lemonade. I remember it distinctly," Quinn insisted. "Even the sky was pink."

"You really believe that, don't you?" Sara asked as she moved the pitcher out of harm's way. "You're in worse shape than I thought. Okay, so it rained pink lemonade. But next time you want something, call me."

Quinn smiled his apology. "You looked so exhausted, I didn't want to waken you."

It had been more than that. The sight of her deep in sleep, the worry lines erased from her forehead, had stirred him to compassion. The hard facade she affected when awake had softened as she slept. She had looked so vulnerable. She was a woman a man wanted to treat with tenderness, to watch over, to care for. Just as she had cared for him, in spite of their argument. He wasn't accustomed to this type of attention. It was a strange feeling, but nice.

He knew he was partly to blame for her exhaustion. Both by his anger and his behavior. "I was supposed to help you, and I'm afraid I've just added to your problems."

"This isn't your fault. You weren't used to working in the sun. For that matter, neither am I. I was about to tell you to quit for the day when I saw you lying on the ground. I should have thought to give you a hat to wear."

"Thanks for the vote of confidence. By the way, it's great of you to take care of me this way." He gestured toward the pitcher. "Do you mind?"

Sara poured him a glass of lemonade, settled the pitcher safely on the nightstand and leaned over to wipe away the few drops of liquid he'd managed to spill on the sheet.

"It's a hell of a note when a guy can't even manage a simple thing like pouring himself a drink, isn't it?" Quinn asked as he lifted the glass to his lips.

"I'm sure you're quite good at pouring drinks," Sara said primly as she handed him the cookie. A teasing smile came over her face. "Maybe the problem is that this is only lemonade."

Quinn gratefully sipped the tangy liquid and considered her statement. "Sam, when I'm back on my feet, I intend to show you a lot of things I'm good at."

"You wish."

"I know," he said quietly as he toasted her with his drink and took a deep swallow. She lowered her eyes and visibly shivered. He was satisfied. She'd gotten his message, just as he had intended her to. He wasn't through with her yet. He sank back into the pillows.

Over the rim of the glass, he noticed there was a change in Sara. Not only had she showered and smelled of fresh lemons, she'd changed into stone-washed jeans and a pink, frilly cotton camisole top. Wisps of freshly washed silken hair had escaped her trademark red ribbon and framed her delicate features. Her shoulders were bare, and a lace bra peeked over the edge of the camisole. When the garment slipped lower and lower and exposed a birthmark, he held his breath.

She looked as good as cotton candy.

He wanted a taste.

The look in Quinn's eyes made Sara feel as if she'd forgotten something when she'd showered and dressed. She fingered the pink ribbon that decorated the front of her brief summer top, checked the zipper on her jeans and ran her hands over her hair to make sure she'd tied it back with a ribbon. Everything was in order, so why did she feel so undressed?

Her eyes met his. The rapt look in his hazel eyes made her blink. Heat swept her from head to toe and wound up in her middle. She could feel herself blush under his scrutiny. The man was a magician, able to make her feel wanton with no more than a heated look. She almost purred like a satisfied kitten.

"Aunt Sara?" The twins were back in the doorway. "The animals ate the cookies you gave them. They're still hungry."

Sara forced herself to turn away from Quinn's frankly admiring gaze. The twins needed her attention more than he did. In their own innocent way, they were telling her it was past time for their breakfast. She'd better go. Preparing a meal was far safer than trading sensual innuendoes with Quinn. "Okay. Tell them to wait until you get dressed. When you're ready, take them downstairs and wait for me. I'll be down as soon as I've made Mr. Tucker comfortable."

Quinn watched Sara refill the glass with lemonade. Far from making him comfortable, Sara's tender loving care was making him decidedly uncomfortable. He shifted uneasily as his body telegraphed the physical reaction he was having just watching her fuss over him.

From the first time he'd seen her, he'd wanted her. He knew it was desire, pure and simple. On the other hand, he thought wryly, it wasn't simple at all. Considering his status around here, it was as complicated as hell.

"Will you be okay until I come back with your breakfast?" Sara asked as she tucked the sheets around him. "I won't be long."

When her hands brushed his skin, Quinn had his doubts, but he nodded wordlessly as she hurried out the door.

He drew a ragged breath. Even though he was only out of jail on a work-furlough with Sara as his jailer, he still wanted her. Wanted her in the way a man wants a desirable woman. It wasn't supposed to happen, but it had and he was damned if he knew what to do about it.

QUINN DOZED while he waited for Sara to come back. Seeing her look so feminine in that frothy top had stirred him in a way beyond physical desire. Until now, he'd always seen her dressed in oversize men's clothing, battling dry dirt and a stubborn mule, wrestling fence rails and trying hard to do a man's job. Today she was all female, the old-fashioned kind a man had to respect. There had been something about her that made him want to play square with her, especially when she had looked so vulnerable in her sleep. And so very, very womanly.

Until today, whenever she'd caught him measuring her up, she'd turned cool, hard as nails. He hadn't cared much about what she thought of him before, but he did now. Especially since she was treating him so tenderly. Not only did she deserve a lot of credit for being so good to him, she deserved a better life than fate had dealt her. What bothered him the most was the worry lines on her forehead that never seemed to go away.

He felt rotten for adding to her burdens.

He had to do something about it. He'd run into enough people who'd gotten through bad times. Maybe one of them could give him advice on how to help Sara. As soon as he was able, he was going to make a telephone call or two.

"Mr. Tucker, when you're better, wanna help us with the garden? Miguel said it was time to tie some more string beans to poles."

Quinn exchanged glances with the twins who were standing in the doorway. "Well, it sounds a heck of a lot easier than digging holes for fence posts. Sure. You can count on me."

It was obvious to Quinn that Jase was anxious to have a man around, and not only for his Aunt Sara. Poor kid, he'd never known a father. Quinn hadn't either, for that matter, and was probably a poor role model for Jase. But, what the hell, there was little harm in stringing up a few plants if it made the kid happy.

Besides, surprisingly enough, he really did get a kick out of being around those two precocious children.

The twins waved goodbye and scrambled downstairs to their breakfast.

Quinn knew it would be at least half an hour before Sara would be back. Until then, the coast was clear. He slowly made his way to the bathroom, freshened up and headed back to bed. Standing on his feet presented more of a challenge than he cared to face.

HUNGER PANGS were getting to him by the time Sara came back carrying a tray with his breakfast. The plate held only a single poached egg on toast, a glass of orange juice and another of milk.

"Looks as if the teddy bear turned his breakfast down," he said as he struggled to sit up against the pillows. "Personally, I could eat a T-bone steak and all the trimmings."

Sara set the tray down and helped him sit up. "Dr. Watkins said to take it easy the first day or so. Not too much food or exercise until you get your strength back. You've had quite a shock to your system."

She was right about that. In fact, his system had received more than one shock. If she only knew that the lemon scent of her as she leaned over him was doing a job on him, too. He swallowed his instinctive reply.

He closed his eyes as Sara's silken ponytail swung over her shoulder and across his forehead. She was Eve, tempting him with her soft beguiling smile, Deliah, goading him with her fragrant scent, Helen of Troy, inspiring him to fight for her attention. He had to do something to put her out of reach.

Conversation. That's it, he thought wildly as she smoothed the sheets around him. Conversation that would take his mind off what she was doing to him.

"Ever been married, Sam?"

"No," she said, shaking her head. "I've managed to avoid that happy state. Have you?"

"No. But you've been engaged."

"Well, yes."

Quinn ran his fingers over the hand that offered him a fork. "What fool let you get away?"

Sara laughed shakily as she disengaged his hand and put the fork down on the tray. Was there no way the man was going to stop making her feel like warm jelly? She sat down in the rocking chair at the side of the bed. "I don't know where this conversation is taking us, but it's really none of your business."

"You don't seem very angry with me for asking."

Surprised at the observation, she returned his quizzical gaze. He was right. She wasn't angry, not at him for asking, or even at her ex-fiancé, Steven, who had been the fool in question. She felt a surge of relief at the realization Steven was in the past where he belonged.

No one had asked her these questions, not since she and her sister, Amy, had shared their demons. No one had cared. From the expression in Quinn's eyes, it looked as if he did. She fixed her eyes on the wallpaper behind the bed and let her mind wander back to another time and another place.

"I know I've mentioned this before, but anyway, I was engaged to a man named Steven Miles. We'd worked together for several years and I thought I'd fallen in love with him."

"You *thought* you fell in love?"

Her eyes met his. "I guess I was ready to fall in love. To have a home and a family. Anyway, we were about to get married when the company we worked for moved back east. It was about the same time that my sister found out she had terminal cancer and asked me to come back here to the family ranch to be with her and take care of the twins. Steven wouldn't have any part of coming here, and I couldn't leave Amy and the children. We wound up going our separate ways."

"And now?" he questioned gently. "How do you feel about him now?"

"I'm glad we broke up. As far as I was concerned, there never was a choice between coming home to Amy and the twins and going with Steven. He was selfish enough to think I would."

Quinn nodded. "I was right, he was a fool."

He lay back against the pillows. "You deserve more from life than you're getting, and I'm not making it any easier for you, am I?" He pushed his untouched plate away. "I guess I wasn't as hungry as I thought I was."

Sara took the tray, put it on the dresser and came back to put her hand against Quinn's forehead. "You feel a little warm. Maybe you'd better try to go back to sleep."

"Every time you look at me that way, Sam, my temperature goes up five degrees. I've had enough of sleeping. It's only making me weaker. I'd much rather talk to you."

"I have to go. There's a lot of work still to be done with the fences."

"You shouldn't be doing it by yourself. It'll wait until I'm back on my feet." He patted the bed. "Stay with me for a while?"

"I can hardly say no. Not when you look at me with eyes that remind me of Jason when he wants me to do something he's afraid I don't want to do." She laughed as she sat on the edge of the bed. "Okay, but only for a few minutes. I haven't cleared up from breakfast."

"It'll wait." He reached for her hand and studied its palm.

"I once tied up with a circus, and a gypsy taught me how to read palms. Want me to read yours?"

"Okay, but just tell me the good things you see. I don't want to know any bad news."

"I see a surprise in your future. No, I don't know what it is, but I do see that you're going to find your heart's desire."

Sara laughed. "Horses to board?"

"Is that your only heart's desire, Sam?"

The tone in his voice was unsettling. She avoided his probing gaze. "Well, yes. For now. That's why you're here, to help me get the ranch ready." Sara drew her hand away. "If that's all you can see, I'd better get back to work. The fences are waiting."

"I wish I felt better so I could help you. Maybe you can hire some help for a few days. Just don't go getting anyone else out of jail. You don't know who you'd draw next time."

Sara looked down at her hands. "I did all right with you." It was the closest she could come to tell him she was sorry for their argument.

"Thanks. And I'd like to apologize for my outburst. You were right. You had every right to be careful."

"I knew you'd never hurt me or the children."

Quinn's heart skipped a beat or two at the tone in her voice. "Not willingly, Sam. Not willingly."

A quick smile covered Sara's face. A dimple danced across her cheek. "I'm never wrong about people, Quinn Tucker." He studied the tempting look on her face and tried to imagine what she would taste like. Sweet, like spun sugar, hot and full of flavor, melting as he swept her mouth with his own.

Sara shifted in her chair. He wondered if she knew he wanted to take her in his arms. But she needn't worry. He was in no condition for wrestling and she wasn't ready for that, either. He tried to concentrate on what she was saying. "You never told me what you do when you're not getting yourself arrested for blocking traffic and resisting arrest."

Considering that he owed her, Sara had the right to know something about him. If she laughed at him for being stupid, so be it. Quinn swallowed his pride.

"Odd jobs here and there. Nothing that would keep me in one place more than a month or two."

"Odd jobs?"

"I've worked for an oil-drilling company in Bakersfield, an aircraft company in San Jose and at the racetracks in Los Angeles a time or two. Oh, and the circus. Nothing special."

"You mean rescuing horses is just a sideline?"

He raised an eyebrow. "Come on, Sam, no fair. That was just an accident. All I did was try to help a poor horse."

"Oh, so you're one of those 'do-gooders.'"

"No more than you…" He was about to defend his position when he saw her lips twitch as she tried to hide a smile. She was teasing him. He liked that. In fact, he admired her sense of humor as much as he admired her… He stopped himself. The whole idea of this conversation was to get his mind off Sara's enchanting body.

"After I had that run-in with Cable, my temper got the better of me. I was in no mood to reason with the jerk, and the discussion got out of hand." He shrugged his shoulders. "It doesn't matter. Getting arrested turned out to be the luckiest thing that could have happened to me."

"Lucky for you? Winding up in jail and being paroled to hard labor is lucky?"

"Well, the way I look at it, meeting up with you and the twins is probably the best thing to happen to me in a long time. Not that I ever gave myself a chance. I never stopped running long enough to enjoy anything or anyone before. Maybe I was running from myself. Anyway, for some reason, things look different to me now. I even like myself a little. I never did before."

"Maybe now you can stop running."

He looked at her. "Maybe. As soon as I find a place to call home."

"Here?"

"The truth is, Sam, I'm not good enough for you, not for the kids, either. I've done things and seen things you wouldn't care to know about. But, I promise, they're behind me now."

He saw tears start to form in the corner of her eyes. "Sam. Come here."

He pulled her down to his embrace, tucked her head under his chin and held her close. "I didn't mean to do this," he said more to himself than her. "I don't deserve you."

He turned her face up to his, outlined her lips with a gentle finger. "I'm going to kiss you again, Sam, if you're not careful."

Sara was drowning in a sea of sensuality. A throbbing began in her middle and was spreading to points north, south, east and west. She could feel Quinn's gaze assessing her, the air surrounding them heavy with desire. As if they had a will of their own, her fingers moved to caress the curls on his chest.

"So, ma'am. It's those curls you like?"

"I'm afraid I like all of you."

"Now, that remark deserves a reward."

His lips met hers in a searching kiss. Soft and tender, then hard and burning. Her lips parted at his urging and she gave herself up to him.

The air was sensually alive with electricity when they parted. She felt it with every breath she took.

"Aunt Sara, when can Mr. Tucker get out of bed?"

Sara jumped up from the bed at the sound of Jase's voice. Grateful for the interruption, she stood and held her hands out to him. "Come on in, sweetheart. Mr. Tucker is getting stronger. He'll be able to come down soon."

"That's good. He promised to help us with the garden."

"He what?"

"Mr. Tucker's going to string the bean plants."

"I'm not sure he's up to gardening, Jase. Maybe another time."

"I'll be up tomorrow, Jase," Quinn broke in. "There are a few other things I want to take care of too, while I'm at it."

"You shouldn't tax your strength. Dr. Watkins said for you to take it easy."

"Stringing up beans and fixing the hinges on the back door doesn't take as much energy as digging those holes, Sam."

"Who's Sam, Mr. Tucker?"

Sara glanced at Quinn and blushed. "Never mind, Jase. It's a private joke between Mr. Tucker and myself."

Quinn gestured to the wooden sword that hung from Jase's belt. "Maybe we can trade stories about warriors while we work in the garden."

"Can we?"

"You bet."

"I'll show you some karate tricks, too, Mr. Tucker."

"Where did you learn about karate?"

"From TV. I'll show you how to save yourself if someone picks a fight with you."

"Too bad I didn't know karate when the sheriff took me on."

"It's good you didn't." Sara broke into the conversation. "You'd probably be serving a long prison sentence instead of a work-furlough program." Sara took the tray and turned to leave. "Come on, Jase."

Quinn had never imagined himself winding up trading fairy tales or taking lessons in self-defense from a four-year-old. He'd been an only child with parents who were too busy for children, and had never looked forward to having any of his own. For that matter, the fact that he seriously thought about children in the first place came as a surprise to him. Maybe it was because Jase and Katie were so irresistible in their innocence, so anxious to be friends.

Then too, there was the way he found himself rediscovering the world through their eyes and wanting to savor every minute of it. It was a world far different than the one he'd known as a child; a second chance at childhood. He watched with appropriate awe as Jase swung the sword in the air in a salute and scampered out of the room.

Quinn glanced over at Sara. Her eyes met and dueled with his. He saw a flash of longing come over her face before she bit her lip and turned away.

"Come back here to me, Sam. We can take up where we left off."

"I don't think it's wise, considering the way the children keep coming in and out, do you?"

"Maybe we can spend some time together later on."

"We'll see. You'd better get some rest. Anyway, with children in the house, it's difficult to—" Sara didn't have time to finish the sentence before he broke in.

"They do go to sleep at night, don't they, Sam?"

Chapter Seven

He swung his legs over the edge of the bed and sat there until his head stopped spinning. Walking gingerly, he made his way to the closet and found trousers and a shirt. Not his, but they would have to do. The dresser yielded vintage underwear, but they would have to do, too. He could visualize what Richard McClintock looked like from the abandoned clothing: medium height, slender, a natty dresser. Too bad his character wasn't as fine a quality as his clothes.

Determined to accompany Sara into town in the morning, he made his plans. He was going to retrieve his suitcase and his truck so he could start to feel better about himself and the way he looked. Even a bound man was entitled to have his own belongings. Then, he intended to take the few bucks he had stashed away in the truck's glove compartment and visit the local drugstore to pick up a few things. Maybe he'd be lucky and there'd be a telephone he could use without Sara knowing.

He winced at the brilliant sunshine streaming in the window. But an overdose of sunshine wasn't going to keep him down. He had things to do.

Dressed, he put a smile on the mirrored image of his face. Wait until Sara saw him in the too-tight pants and a shirt that strained across his muscled chest. Before he headed out, he checked the shirt buttons. They were on the verge of popping out of the buttonholes, but for now, they were all fastened. Sara wouldn't have anything to complain about.

Barefoot, he slowly made his way downstairs.

"Breakfast or lunch?" Sara asked from behind the refrigerator door.

"Anything substantial as long as it isn't something the stuffed dog turned down."

He could hear her laughter as she continued to search.

"How about a grilled cheese sandwich? Children love them."

"Sam, in case you haven't noticed, I'm not a child."

Sara stopped in the act of closing the refrigerator door. The man in the sexy, tight trousers and the muscle-bound shirt was definitely not a child. She stared at the dark curls that were escaping his gaping shirt, at the long tapered fingers that were trying to refasten buttons that kept slipping from straining buttonholes. Rolled-up sleeves revealed bare, tanned arms. His cheeks had turned a golden brown from days working in the sun. An ebony curl hung over roguish eyes. She smothered a sigh.

No, Quinn Tucker was definitely not a child.

She stilled the physical desire that flooded her and was thankful for the refrigerator door that shielded her from his twinkling hazel eyes. "Chicken salad sandwich, and that's my last offer. Take it or leave it."

"I'll take it."

There was something in his voice as his gaze swept her that told her he wasn't only talking about sandwiches.

Sara took inventory of her emotions while she busied herself making lunch. Now that she was no longer hurt or angry, she was willing to admit she *was* highly attracted to Quinn. She enjoyed his company, his sexual innuendoes, his teasing, his quirky smile. He was an intensely alive man, but she suspected he was the kind who toyed with a woman's affection for the fun of it.

She reined in her thoughts. After all, what would it all add up to? A week or two of trying to satisfy a need to be held and loved and then, goodbyes? Her experience with Steven had taught her that when making love, love didn't necessarily have anything to do with it. How else could she explain Steven's casual departure, his flippant remark that she could keep his ring as something to remember him by?

Then, there was the example of her brother-in-law, Richard McClintock. He hadn't looked back, either, when he'd left Amy and the newborn twins. She didn't want to be like her sister, doomed to be attracted to a man who couldn't love and cherish one woman for any length of time. For all she knew, Quinn was that kind of a man.

"Here you go." She set a plate in front of him, added another of sliced tomatoes and cucumbers, and poured a fresh glass of pink lemonade.

"Join me?"

"Can't. I promised the kids I'd bake this afternoon. I want to get started before it gets too hot."

As far as Sara was concerned, it was already too hot in the kitchen. She had to do something to escape Quinn's studied glances, even if it meant baking cookies in ninety-degree heat.

What she really wanted was to have Quinn help her bake the cookies. To join her in another heart-to-heart conversation while she stirred up the batter, to lick the spoon, maybe even to share its taste with him. But she couldn't trust herself to stay out of his arms.

"It's pretty hot here. Maybe you'd like to go outside. There's a hammock under the apple tree, if you'd like to rest for a while. It doesn't pay to overdo it."

Quinn started to turn down the offer. He was enjoying the domestic picture Sara made as she pulled out the ingredients for baking. Enough to pull her into his arms and plant that kiss he had stored up, right on her cute turned-up nose. Until he remembered his determination not to tempt her into his arms until he was a free man. He thought of the well-worn cliché, "if you can't stand the heat, get out of the kitchen." It was already too hot in here. He'd better leave before he was tempted to put his thoughts into action. He was in no shape to engage in any sexual horseplay, even if he wanted to.

"I think I will go out, at least until it gets too hot to stay out there."

"Wait a minute until I get your shoes. They're still in the parlor."

She brought Quinn's penny loafers and knelt at his feet. Her lemon-scented hair fell forward and exposed the nape of her neck as it curved down into her blouse. An urge to taste her honey-colored skin made him catch his breath. He was tempted to throw caution to the winds, draw her up into his lap and kiss her until both of them were satisfied. No, not satisfied. He wanted more than a kiss. Instead he took a deep breath and waved her away. "I'm a big boy now, Sam, remember?"

How could she forget? Had it only been yesterday that she'd washed his bare torso to revive him and felt sensations she only dimly remembered? Crimson, she pointed to the door. "Out!"

Throwing her a wicked smile, he stood and wiggled his feet into his shoes. Raised eyebrows told her he knew exactly what she was feeling. The movement of his lithe hips as he crossed the kitchen sent hot waves of desire through her. It's a good thing he's leaving, she thought. If he kept this up, she'd never get around to the cookies.

"Out, out, out!"

She waited until he'd exited the kitchen before she trusted herself to follow him to the screened door. Jase and Katie's shouts of welcome brought a wistful smile to her lips. Their giggles as Quinn pretended to shadowbox with them, both at the same time, was heartwarming. When he put his arms around the twins and leaned over to look at what Jase was offering, she sighed. There was no doubt about it, the children needed a man in their lives. A man like Quinn Tucker.

"MR. TUCKER, want to see what I've got?"

"Sure."

Jase picked up a tiny mongrel pup and thrust it at him. If it had known better days, they were long gone. The dog blinked at Quinn, then settled into a mournful stare.

"Where'd you get that?" Quinn cautiously reached out and patted the dog's head.

"Miguel found him for me. It was sittin' in the middle of the road."

"Are you sure it doesn't belong to someone?"

"Miguel saw him sittin' there yesterday, too, so he brought him home. I've already named my stuffed dog Shelby. What do you think I should call this one?"

"Well," Quinn pretended to study the dog. "He looks like a Prince to me."

"Gee, that's great. I'll call him Prince. Do you think he's hungry?"

"I'll bet he is." Quinn stared into the dog's eyes. It had obviously been abandoned and left alone to starve. "Yep, he sure looks hungry. Why don't you go on in and get some bread and milk until we can get some dog food. You can feed him while your aunt decides what to do with him.''

"Gee, thanks, Mr. Tucker. I'll bet you know a lot about dogs!''

Quinn swept Jase's bangs off his forehead. "Not much. Never had one of my own. But I can a spot a hungry look when I see one.''

"Wow! Hold him for me, Mr. Tucker. I'll be right back.''

He ran into the house. "Got to get some bread and milk for my new dog, Aunt Sara.''

"New dog? What new dog?''

"The one Mr. Tucker is holding for me.''

Sara went to the screen door. Sure enough, there were Quinn and Katie, examining a black-and-white spotted puppy. Before she had a chance to question Jase, he shot past her holding a loaf of bread, a bottle of milk and a bowl.

"Wait a minute, Jase. You're not going to feed a dog from one of my dishes!''

It was too late. Quinn and the children were filling the dish. The starving animal was squeezing between them and nipping at their hands to get at the food.

Sara gave up. She'd find out about the dog later. It was the picture of Quinn and the twins that fascinated her. Children had a way of judging character, she thought as she watched the happy scene. It certainly looked as if Quinn had passed the test. The man was a charmer, all right.

Quinn was the type of a man Jase needed. Too bad he'd said he wasn't the kind to put down roots.

EARLY THE NEXT MORNING, Sara laid out her shopping list and the money that would have to last her for the rest of the month. The sale of her engagement ring had paid the taxes for the year, otherwise they'd be living on rice and beans and what they grew in the small kitchen garden Miguel and the children tended.

She bit her lip as she studied the short list. Her heart sank as she glanced at the small pile of bills on the table. There was no way she was going to be able to buy everything she needed. Ready money was short and would be until she started to board horses. She crossed out several of the items that would have to wait until the twins' next social security check would arrive. Thank goodness the ranch was clear and the taxes low enough to handle. And for Miguel, bless him, who worked largely for room and board.

Her own savings account was low, too low. It would have to go for hay and supplies, once she could get some horses to board. Short of finding a part-time job in town, she didn't know where the money for extras would come from. The job would have to wait until the twins were in school, but that was still almost two months away.

Since she and Quinn had almost finished fencing the ranch before he'd gotten ill, it was time to post a notice in the general store. She knew that her chances were slim to none that anyone wanted to board horses, but it was the only idea she'd been able to come up with. If only there was an easier, quicker way out.

The scent of Quinn's shaving lotion mingled with the lingering smell of yesterday's gingerbread. She looked up in time to see a frown cross his face as he came to a halt before her.

"Breakfast?" She started to gather the lists and the money.

Quinn put his hand over hers. "Going shopping?"

"Yes. I'm going into town as soon as the twins come back from gathering eggs."

"Eggs?"

Sara looked uncomfortable. "What we don't eat, I barter for groceries at the general store."

"Barter. I see." Quinn saw too much. Sara was making ends meet the hard way. His glance strayed to the shopping list on the table. "Do you mind?" He picked up the paper and quickly noted the crossed out items, items clearly intended for Jase and Katie and that Sara had considered expendable.

"Sara Ann Martin, it looks to me as if you really can't afford me. Oh, I know." He held up his hand when she started to interrupt him. "I came cheaper than most hired hands, but then I'm not hired, am I?"

"I thought we settled all that. I thought we'd put the reason you're here behind you. I even thought we'd become friends."

She was still his jailer, no matter how friendly they'd become, Quinn thought as he studied the list. He had to do something to change all that.

"I'm coming into town with you," he said firmly as he handed Sara the piece of paper.

"Are you sure you feel strong enough? Maybe you'd better stick around the house."

"Afraid I'll escape?" It wasn't easy for him to have to ask for permission to do anything, but he'd be damned if he was going to let Sara go into town alone.

"Okay, have it your way. Come along, but I don't know what you're going to do in town."

"Get my sunglasses out of my truck, for starters."

"The sheriff won't—"

"Yes, he will, if you ask him to." Frustrated, Quinn ran his hands through his hair. "For Pete's sake, Sam, I'm not asking for the truck. Just my sunglasses."

He stood there, hands on his hips, hating to beg, hoping she wouldn't push him too far. He was going to town with or without her permission. His felt his temper gather like a dark pressure behind his jaw.

"Come on, then. I'll get Miguel to watch Jase and Katie. We won't be gone long." Sara gestured to the coffeepot warming on the back of the stove. "Help yourself to coffee and gingerbread. I'll meet you at the truck."

Quinn swallowed the coffee in deep drafts. Anxious to get started, he fought to stay calm. It would take a cool head to accomplish what he wanted to do without letting Sara know. He stuffed several gingerbread men in his shirt pocket for later and joined Sara outside in the truck.

He took greater note of his surroundings on the way to Juniper than he had two weeks ago. The effects of the prolonged drought were obvious everywhere. From the looks of things, he doubted that any of the ranches they passed were doing any better than the Lazy M. Several had For Sale signs posted, a few advertised horses to rent or board. A newly painted sign advertised bed and breakfast. There wasn't a sign of life anywhere. He shook his head. Sara Ann Martin wasn't going to find many takers for her horse bed and breakfast.

Juniper was quiet. A small group of men stood talking outside the barber shop, several disappeared into the general store. The tiny park with its dry tiled fountain was deserted. One or two townspeople hurried along the boardwalk.

"Not much doing in town, is there?" he asked Sara.

"It's too early in the year for tourism. Fall is Juniper's best season."

Quinn was glad. It would make his presence easier if there were few people around to notice him.

They drew up in front of Juniper's jailhouse. He could see Sara was troubled as she gazed at him. She started to speak, put her hand on his arm. His muscles tensed at her touch. His face set, his lips formed a thin line; he was girded for bear.

"Let me do the talking," Sara said quietly.

The look he shot her would have intimidated a lesser woman, but Sara was obviously out to prevent bloodshed. His blood.

She went into the jail.

Quinn swallowed his pride and followed.

Sheriff Cable glanced up from the game of solitaire spread across his desk. He laid down the cards and rose to his feet. "Howdy, Ms. Martin. Had enough of this guy? Ready to turn him in?"

Quinn felt the blood drain from his face.

Sara shook her head in warning.

"Not at all, Sheriff. Mr. Tucker has been a model hand. We just stopped by to get his sunglasses from his truck."

"And my suitcase," Quinn added between clenched teeth. "I need some clean clothes."

The sheriff circled Quinn and broke into a loud laugh. "You sure do. Looks as if you've borrowed clothes from a runt."

"They're Richard McClintock's clothing, Sheriff. You can see why Mr. Tucker needs his own clothes."

Cable scratched his head. "Well, I dunno. Judge Andrews ordered the truck and the suitcase impounded until Tucker's sentence is up. About two more weeks, I guess. Judge figured it was the only way to make certain Tucker stayed put and worked off his sentence."

Sara gave Cable her best smile. "I'll take full responsibility, Sheriff."

"Well, I guess it'll be okay. The car's down at Bob Foster's garage. I'll call and tell him you're coming." He leered at Quinn. "You can't have the keys, mister. I'm not that dumb." He thought a moment. "Oh yeah, the glove compartment has a combination lock, don't it? Couldn't figure it out, myself.''

Clenching and unclenching his fists, Quinn glared at the sheriff. "Tried it, did you?''

Sara grabbed Quinn's arm and pulled him toward the door. "Let's go, Mr. Tucker. I have a lot to do.''

Back in the sunlight, Sara pointed to the garage at the end of the street. "Go get what you need and I'll meet you back at the general store. I'd go with you but I don't want to leave the eggs out in the sun too long.''

Quinn glanced back at the jailhouse door, nodded curtly and took off. Swearing under his breath, he made his way to the garage where a tall, gangly man waited for him.

"You Quinn Tucker? The sheriff said you'd be by.'' Foster appraised Quinn. "You sure don't look like a criminal, but he said to keep an eye on you just the same.''

Quinn ignored the man and headed for the truck parked alongside the garage. Its bright red paint was covered with dust, and a large cat and three kittens had made their home on the front seat. To the mother's displeasure, Quinn opened the door and lifted out the kittens. With a snarl, the mother cat sprang out to protect her litter, but not before she took a swipe at Quinn. Sucking the blood off the back of his hand, Quinn chalked up one more grievance against Juniper, its judge and its sheriff. As for the mother cat, she was just being protective. Since he'd met Sara, Jase and Katie, he could appreciate that.

He worked the combination lock of the glove compartment and reached inside for his sunglasses. Glancing around to make certain he wasn't being watched too closely, he slid his automobile registration and a small amount of currency into his pocket.

After a brief conversation with Foster, Quinn waved and took off for the drugstore.

The store's shades were drawn, the dim interior cool and private.

"Something I can do for you? We're about to close for noon, but..." The druggist put his smock back on.

Using the telephone for a private conversation was now out of the question. Quinn shrugged. "I'm looking for some cologne. Charlie."

"Right here." The druggist led the way to the perfume counter. "New around here, or just passing through?"

"Passing through," Quinn answered, as he noticed a stack of disposable cameras and handed one to the man. "Any chance you can wrap it for me?" He hadn't been on the receiving end of many presents to judge how they should look, but he wanted these to look nice. He watched while they were wrapped in bright floral paper and tied with red ribbon.

"For someone special?" the druggist asked as he handed over the packages.

"Very." Quinn clamped his lips shut. The druggist shrugged and took the money offered him.

Quinn was standing by the truck waiting for Sara when she appeared.

"Please go on in and bring out the packages Dave Markus has waiting. I'll be along as soon as I post this." She showed him a notice that the Lazy M was open for boarding horses.

He nodded and went into the store. Ignoring curious glances, he gathered Sara's purchases and left. He slipped his own small packages in with the groceries. When he returned, Sara was seated in the truck, and the notice was posted on the store's bulletin board. Along with a dozen others, he noticed as he passed. Times were obviously bad in Juniper.

The drive back to the Lazy M was made in silence. Quinn kept glancing at Sara. The worry lines on her forehead were deeper. He didn't think she was any more confident about her business enterprise than he was.

When they reached the ranch, he carried the box of groceries into the kitchen.

She started to empty the box and picked up a small, brightly wrapped package. "Oh dear, Dave gave me someone else's package by mistake."

"Really?" Quinn made a great show of peering at the package. "Why don't you open it and see?"

"I can't do that. It doesn't belong to me. I'll return it the next time I go into town."

He pretended to read over her shoulder. "What does the card say?"

"'To Jase and Katie so you can take pictures of Prince,'" she read and eyed Quinn in surprise. "It's from you! What is it?"

"Just a camera. I thought they'd have some fun with it."

"You shouldn't have spent your money that way."

"Why not? Money is meant to be enjoyed. I enjoyed buying that for the twins. Open the other one."

Sara unwrapped a bottle of her favorite cologne. "Oh, Quinn. I don't know how to thank you."

"Don't try."

"And what's this?" Sara pointed to the neat row of bills nested on the table.

"Last time I asked, they called it fifty-dollar bills."

"Do they come from you, too?"

"Yes," he said, avoiding her eyes.

She regarded him with suspicion. "Where on earth did you get all that money?"

He had to tell her. She'd find out anyway. "I sold my truck to Foster."

"Sold your truck!"

"Yes. It wasn't worth very much, and I didn't need it for the next couple of weeks."

Sara shook her head. "I can't take money from you."

Quinn folded his arms across his chest and leaned against the kitchen sink. Damn the woman's pride!

"I owe you two hundred and fifty dollars. The extra fifty is for the trouble I've caused you lately."

"You didn't need to do that."

"Yes, I did."

"I don't have the power to lift your sentence, Quinn. It's not just the money."

"I know." Quinn straightened and came toward her. "I have to feel like a free man."

The look in Quinn's eyes took her breath away. "Why is it so important to you?" she whispered as a lump rose in her throat.

"So I could do this. And so you can't accuse me of taking advantage of you. Ever."

He pulled her into his arms and, forgetting everything but the way he wanted her, kissed her fiercely until she melted against him.

THE NIGHT COULDN'T COME quickly enough for Quinn. The glances he'd exchanged with Sara throughout the afternoon had been full of promises, promises he intended to keep.

After Sara had tucked the twins in bed, she came downstairs to where Quinn was waiting for her. He took her into his arms and gazed into her eyes. "I want you, Sam. I think you want me, too."

At her shy nod, he swung her into his arms and carried her upstairs. "Your bedroom or mine?"

"Yours has the double bed."

"Ah, Sam, that's one of the things I like about you. You're so damn honest." He carried her into his room, to the bed that waited for them. He hesitated. "I don't suppose you..." Mute, Sara shook her head. "Hang loose for a moment, I'll be right back."

He rummaged in his suitcase, put a foil-wrapped package on the nightstand and joined her.

The moon was splashing through the windows as he carefully unbuttoned her shirt, slid it down and kissed each shoulder as it was exposed to his lips. She felt a deep flush sweep over her, felt her breasts harden. When his gaze met hers, she was swept into touching, tasting, holding him. A sweet thrill blurred her senses. He slid his hands over her hips, fitting her body to his. She drew back to look at him, not prepared to let her fears go.

Quinn smiled into her eyes. "Look at me, Sam. Look at me as if you were looking in a mirror. What do you see?"

She gazed at him and reached to trace the encouraging smile that curved his mouth. His hazel eyes turned smoky with the same desire that throbbed through her. She had never felt beautiful before, but she did now. She stroked his face, touched his lips. Secure in the knowledge that he was a man who wanted her happiness, she answered, "I see a woman who wants the man holding her."

"Are you sure, Sam?"

She nodded wordlessly.

Awash with tenderness, Quinn drew aside the rest of her clothing, brushed her skin with his warm hands, cupped her breasts and kissed each one reverently. "So beautiful," he murmured as he slid his hands over her bare flesh. No one had the right to have such silken skin, he thought as he gazed down at her. He couldn't get enough of the taste, the feel of her. She was driving him to a point where he was fast losing his self-control.

"You were made to be loved, Sam. Let me love you."

They sank against the pillows, his urgent touch spanning Sara's waist and moving lower, suffusing her with heat. Awash in a sea of longing, she gathered him into her arms. When he came to her and murmured soft words of approval, she drew his lips to hers, touched the tip of her tongue to his. For a moment, his tongue dueled with hers.

He whispered words of encouragement, moving his hands lower, nudging her legs apart. She welcomed the hands that caressed her, the lips that moved along her skin to her waist, her hip, her thigh. A delicious heat washed over her as he traced the hollow of her hips and moved to touch the core of her. When he joined his body to hers, a rainbow of brilliant colors formed behind her closed eyelids.

When he held her face with newly work-roughened hands and delved into her mouth, she let herself be led into his magical world. She needed him as much as he seemed to need her, needed him to fill the emptiness that had been her companion for so long. He had asked for a place in her life; she would give it to him.

His arms were strong, his body hard and hot as he exorcised the past, offered her a new beginning. She let herself go, felt the emptiness vanish in the wake of passion-filled moments.

LOVEMAKING HAD ALMOST been a game to him, until now, Quinn thought, but it hadn't taken him long to realize that Sara fit into his life like a missing piece of a puzzle. She was a one-man woman, caring and loving, soft and strong at the same time.

As he held her close to him, his thoughts strayed back through the weeks since he'd been paroled into her custody. Ironically, even though he'd somehow known she played for keeps, it hadn't stopped him from teasing her into an awareness of her attractiveness, her own sexuality. It was more than a physical desire he felt for her. He knew that now. It was her courage, strength and dedication to her adopted family that fascinated him and made him look at her in a way that was new to him.

To tell the truth, like any man, in the first ninety seconds after he'd seen her he'd responded with physical desire. Now, he felt far more. No other woman had been able to make him question his commitment to personal independence.

He buried his face in her fragrance. He wanted to keep her in his arms in the worst way. He wanted to taste the sweetness of her lips again and again. To finger each silken thread of her golden hair, to slide his hands over her bare skin, to feel her heart beat under his hands. To share again the passion that had put a contented smile on her face. To make her feel safe.

Sara nestled in his arms, content. All was right with her world. But was it wise to let the passion within her explode? Even though his fingers were hot as they rolled pulsing ripples of pleasure through her face and arms, she knew Quinn was still a rolling stone and might not be meant for her.

Dimly, within her passion, Sara felt a sadness. The knowledge that he was going to leave in two weeks kept her from telling him how she felt. The hurt of Steven's desertion flared anew. She rested her head on his chest. "This doesn't make any difference, does it? You're still going to leave. I can't go through losing you."

"I'm not your Steven, Sara," he said quietly. "This is Quinn Tucker holding you. I don't promise anything but the best I have to give until the day I leave. I haven't lied about that. I won't take anything you don't want to give."

Sara leaned against his chest. His body warmth sent a glow through her, his hard strength both welcome and frightening, his male scent intoxicating. She wanted more of him. When he kissed her again, so deeply she felt he was reaching into her very soul, she was almost lost. His arms were reassuring, comforting. The doubts she had as to where this might be taking her faded into the background. She needed, wanted Quinn more than she'd ever wanted a man before. Nothing that had gone before this moment had affected her in this way; she was certain nothing she would experience in the future would, either.

"Sam? Come on back from wherever you've gone. Time is too precious to spend like this. Make love with me."

Passion sprang to life once again, thrusting her into a world where only the two of them existed.

THE NIGHT HAD BEEN ALL she'd dreamed of, a joy she had never experienced until now. She smelled the musky scent of him on her body and thought with a rueful smile of how much she enjoyed the warm cocoon of his body twined around her, his arm thrown over her.

Through the open window, the day was dawning. She felt a pang of regret that the night was over. She didn't dare let herself be found with him. She shouldn't have allowed herself to be drawn into the night's sensuality, but she'd had to taste the love he offered her.

"Quinn, I have to go. The twins will be awake soon."

"Ah, yes, and the stuffed animals who are always hungry. Remember me, Sam," he whispered before she slid out of bed and tore herself away.

Remember him? How could she forget?

Chapter Eight

Later that morning, Sara gazed at the money Quinn had left on the table. "I can't take it," she said, handing it back to him. "Not after you sold your truck. You won't have any money left for yourself."

"Take the money, Sam," Quinn insisted. He folded her hands over the bills. "I won't feel free until you do."

A wave of apprehension swept over Sara. She looked up into his smoky, hazel eyes. "Free? Does that mean you're leaving?" *After last night?*

"No, not yet. My sentence isn't over, is it? Besides, I still have a few things I promised myself I'd take care of around here." He wrapped his arms around her and kissed the nape of her neck.

"You're sure?"

"I'm sure. I intend to stay for the balance of my sentence, Sam. It's just that I have to *feel* free. A bound man wouldn't have the right to hold you this way, or love you the way I did last night."

Eyes sparkling, Sara turned and nestled in his arms. "You're behaving like a fool. I've never thought of you as a bound man. Not after the first day, anyway. You've come to mean a great deal to me and to the twins. And even to Miguel." She stroked a curl away from his forehead, caressed his cheek. "But I can't let you stay without paying you for your time."

"You already have, Lemonade Angel," he whispered against her hand. "You already have."

"I have? How?"

"When you saved my life. Tradition has it I belong to you now."

Sara's heart ached for him. Quinn was a proud man, had suffered the indignity of being "sold" to her. Aside from the first few days of temper, he had even kept his wounded ego from showing. She knew how much he valued his pride and his freedom. To have him offer them to her was a gift beyond compare.

"I don't know who belongs to whom, anymore. Not after last night. But I do know I'm very grateful to you." She offered him her lips and was rewarded by a kiss that stirred her senses once again. Would she ever get enough of this man?

"Funny how you always taste like lemonade, Sam," he said, hugging her tight. "And how you manage to look like an innocent angel, no matter what you do." He stroked her hip with urgent hands. "Or what you wear."

"Not so innocent." Remembering the lovemaking in the dark of the night, she blushed. What must he think of her?

"I wouldn't have you any other way," he said, as if reading her thoughts.

Sara was mesmerized by his deep, melodious voice. As heat suffused her, she answered, "Only with you, Quinn. Only with you."

"Thank you, Sam."

"For what?"

"For making me such a lucky man."

"I'm lucky, too." She gave in to the urge to unbutton his shirt. Her fingers seemed to have a will of their own as they fingered the curls on his chest. She bent to kiss his flesh. He tasted every bit as good as he had last night, warm, alive. "You must have been sent by my guardian angel to prove to me that good men really exist."

Good? Quinn felt a rush of regret for what he'd been, what he'd done. And what he'd missed. "I'll try to live up to that, but I haven't been—"

"No 'buts.'" She covered his lips with her hand. "It's what you are now that counts."

Oblivious to their surroundings, they locked in an embrace.

"Well, well, what do we have here?"

Sara froze. Her heart plummeted to her stomach, left her with a pain she hadn't felt for a long time. It was the voice she'd hoped never to hear again. Richard McClintock had come back. He was her worst nightmare come true.

She'd only seen her brother-in-law twice in seven years, at her sister's wedding and when the twins were born. Now, dressed in the height of fashion as if money were no object, he stood in the doorway as if he owned the place. His tailored white Panama suit fit his small frame as though it had been made for him. Fake lizard boots covered his feet. A paisley tie lay against a melon-colored silk shirt. As he moved his hand to rub his chin, a diamond ring flashed on his right hand. Raised eyebrows and a knowing smile covered his face. She could tell by the way his eyes darted from her to Quinn that he read only the worst possible explanation into Quinn's presence. "Richard McClintock! Where did you come from? Why are you here?"

"What difference does it make? I've come home." His mocking gaze lingered on Quinn. "From the looks of things, I'm just in time."

Quinn clenched his fists. He felt the blood drain from his face as he regarded the man in the doorway. It didn't take a genius to know that the stranger was referring to him. The smirk on McClintock's face set off a fire alarm in Quinn. There was trouble ahead. He knew it from looking at the man as surely as he knew Sara's stories about the man were true. It was all he could do to keep from punching that sly smile off his face. He took a deep breath.

Sara put a restraining hand on his arm. "Quinn, this is Richard McClintock, my brother-in-law."

"I heard all about you." McClintock smirked at Quinn. "Jailbird, aren't you?"

"Who he is is none of your business. I asked you, what do you want?"

McClintock shot Sara a deprecating grin. "I haven't had any breakfast. I could use some home cooking." Grabbing a chair, he turned it around and straddled it. "How about a cup of coffee and anything else you've got around here that's worth eating?"

"You'll get breakfast when hell freezes over!" Quinn took a step forward. "Get your carcass out of here."

The men eyed each other. Tension crackled in the air. Sara pushed Quinn out of the way. "Let me handle this. All you're going to get out of me is a good-bye, Richard McClintock. I want you out of here now!"

"Hey, wait a minute!" His face red with indignation, McClintock stood and drew himself up to his full height. "I have just as much right to be here as you do, Sara. This is my home as well as yours. I'm not leaving!"

"Too bad you didn't remember it was your home four years ago when the children were born, or when Amy died and the children needed their father. As far as I'm concerned, you forfeited any right you might have had to the ranch when you deserted Amy and the twins."

"Aw, come on. I just left to make some money. I always intended to come back. Something always seemed to come up. Heard you had company, thought I'd check him out." He gestured to Quinn and smiled. "It's a good thing I did."

"How did you hear..." Sara's voice trailed off. She balled up her fists and marched up to McClintock. "You've been in touch with your cousin, Judge Andrews, haven't you?"

"So what?"

"Are you saying Lester Andrews knew where you were all this time?"

"I kept in touch. Family and all that, you know."

"How convenient of you to remember family. Well, let me tell you, your family was here! They needed you, especially when Amy took sick. You could at least have come back when my sister died! Surely Andrews told you about her passing?"

"I'm no good at funerals."

"You're no good at anything else, either. You had little children who needed you."

"They had you. Besides, I wouldn't have known what to do with babies. Lester said you were doing okay. You didn't need me."

"How would he know?" Sara's voice shook with anger. "The only good thing that man ever did for me was to place Quinn on a work-furlough program to work for me. That didn't stop him from making me pay Quinn's fine, first," she said bitterly. "Chivalry must run in your family."

"Well, you got yourself a man around the house, didn't you?"

"Get your mind out of the gutter. Quinn Tucker works for me, nothing else."

"Yeah, sure." McClintock glanced at Quinn. "I found you in this guy's arms, didn't I? Talking about children, where are the little squirts, anyway?"

Quinn stiffened. "You don't need to know. Now listen to Sara and get the hell out of here!"

"Sara, is it? First names and kissing privileges come with the parole?"

"Richard, I want you out of here!" Sara marched to the kitchen door and flung it open. "Get out, now!"

"You're not very welcoming to a man in his own home. I'm not going!"

"It'll be a cold day in hell before this is your home again," Quinn interjected.

"Who in the blazes do you think you are?" McClintock shot back, carefully keeping his distance. "From the looks of it, I'd say you're much more than a hired hand around here, but that don't cut anything with me."

"Aunt Sara? Mr. Tucker?"

Quinn swung around to meet the frightened eyes of Jase and Katie. "It's okay, kids. But maybe you two ought to go back outside."

Katie whimpered and buried her face in Sara's arms.

Jase took a brave step toward Quinn. "We came in for breakfast, Mr. Tucker," he said as he eyed his father warily. "We didn't know you had company."

"I ain't company, squirt. I'm your father. Grown some, haven't you?"

Jase didn't look too happy with the announcement. He looked at Quinn for confirmation.

Quinn reluctantly nodded and held out his hand for Jase to hold.

McClintock snorted. "What else are you around here besides a hired hand?"

"If you don't get out of here now, you're one rooster who's going to get his wings clipped, if I have anything to say about it."

Quinn rested his hand on Jase's shoulder. He could feel the boy trembling beneath the thin cotton shirt. Even though he would have liked to punch the louse out, he had to put an end to the argument for the twins' sake.

"I'll be outside, Sara. Call me if you need me." He shot McClintock a warning look and led Jase and the tearful Katie out the door. "You'd better be gone when I come back," he said over his shoulder. "And if you're smart, you won't wait around until I do."

McClintock's gaze darted to Sara. "Don't know why you hold my leaving against me. I'm not a family man. Amy knew that."

"My sister didn't get pregnant by herself."

"Hey, one kid would have been bad enough to take, but twins!"

"I'd tell you to go to the devil, Richard Mc-Clintock, but even the devil wouldn't have you!"

"Aw, Sara. You look so cute when you're riled up. Just like Amy. Not that I minded. It was fun making up."

Sara shifted in disgust. "Get out of here!"

"Better watch it, Miss High-and-Mighty, or I'll tell Lester about how cozy you and that jailbird are. When I get through, he'll take the kids away from you and give them to me. The ranch, too."

"Lester Andrews may be a judge, but he's rotten through and through, just like you. Out!"

"I'm going, but don't think you're rid of me. I'll be watching you."

THEIR RELATIONSHIP had changed. With a sinking feeling, Quinn knew from the first troubled glance Sara gave him over dinner that he was back to square one with her. Not that he blamed her. With her brother-in-law back in the picture, everything had changed. Whatever direction their new relationship would have taken, there were more important things to take care of right now. Everything else would have to wait.

He'd overheard McClintock's threat, knew that protecting the twins and their share of the ranch from their father came first with her. Just as it now came first with him. He felt a wave of tenderness shoot through him whenever he met Sara's troubled eyes.

More than anything in the world, he wanted to protect her, make her feel safe.

He was troubled, too, but he tried to be realistic. There was little he could do for her and the twins, except put the fear of God into McClintock for now. But when he left, who would watch over them? Who would keep McClintock from taking over? Especially, if he had his cousin the judge on his side.

It came as a surprise to him that he thought of Sara and the children as his responsibility. But he did, and the thought was heavy on his conscience. As far as Sara knew, he was, after all, passing through her life. At least, that had been his game plan a few weeks ago. Now, he wasn't so sure. So what did he expect? She wasn't the type to keep a man who wanted to go. Not his Sam. She was too proud. He drummed his fingers on the table, waiting to have an excuse to go upstairs where he could do some serious thinking.

The twins chattered noisily. Jase boasted he had taught Prince to beg for food. Katie described the pictures she had taken with the new camera Quinn had brought back from town. Through it all, Sara nodded at appropriate times, but he could tell her mind was elsewhere. The kids may have forgotten their father's visit, but not their aunt.

"Don't you care for meat loaf?" Another worry line crinkled Sara's forehead as she frowned at Quinn's untouched plate. "I can make you something else, if you like. A sandwich?"

"No, I mean, yes. Your meat loaf is great. I'm not very hungry." Liar, he thought as his stomach growled at the spicy smell of the salsa-covered offering and the steamed rice and boiled vegetables that filled the table. It was just that he couldn't keep his mind on eating. He was filled with impotent anger knowing that Richard McClintock's appearance jeopardized Sara and the twins and that he hadn't figured out a way to protect them.

"I'll put your plate in the warming oven. It's the first time since I've known you that you weren't ready to eat." She reached across the table to feel his hand. "You don't feel warm. I hope you haven't had a relapse. You might have overdone it today."

Quinn couldn't meet her anxious eyes or bring himself to draw his hand away. The last thing he wanted was to add to her problems, but he needed to have some contact with her. If only to reassure himself she was all right. "I feel fine, really. Just not hungry," he reassured her. "How about you?"

"I'm mad as hell," she said in a low voice so the children couldn't hear. "I'd give anything if only Richard hadn't come back."

"Mad is good, but don't let it get you down."

Her glance darted to the twins. She shook her head and motioned him to silence. "I'll try not to, but it's not going to be easy. I never could stand the man. But I can handle it. It won't be the first time."

Shortly after dinner, he pleaded exhaustion, excused himself and went upstairs to bed. Washing up in the bathroom, he was hit with the realization that, no matter what kept him and Sam apart, the scent of lemons would remind him of her forever.

Sometime during the night, Quinn realized he hadn't heard Sara go into her room after she'd put the twins to bed. He stepped into his jeans, grabbed his shirt and made his way downstairs.

"Sam?" He found her sitting at the kitchen table, tears sliding down her cheeks. He crouched by her side and put his arm around her. "What's the matter?"

"I hate to admit it, but I guess I'm afraid."

"Afraid, Sam? What do you have to be afraid of?"

"Richard, and what he might do. I couldn't bear it if he took the children away from me, or got part of the ranch. He'd only try to sell it, and the children would be left without anything. I don't have the money to buy him out, either." She took a deep breath when he started to speak. "We have to be careful. I can't give him a reason to take the children away."

"Sounded to me as if he didn't care much about the twins. Maybe it's just the ranch he wants."

"Over my dead body. He's not going to get it. Nor his cousin, Judge Andrews, neither. Andrews has offered to buy the ranch from me more than once."

"What would he want with it?"

"It would have been a good investment if he could have gotten it dirt cheap. He's been like a bird of prey, just watching and waiting for me to give up. And now, Richard's back doing the same thing."

He rose, moved behind her and cupped her shoulders with his warm, broad hands. He gently massaged them in small circular motions. "Relax. You don't have to worry about the judge tonight. Tell me about McClintock. He doesn't look like much, certainly not enough to be a threat."

"He is. He always was." She wiped the tears from her cheeks. "He first showed up here about six years ago, to visit his cousin. From the first moment he laid eyes on my sister, he was after her. She was so pretty, so innocent, so flattered by his attention. He told her about the wonderful world out there just waiting for her, that she was wasted here in Juniper. Told her he'd show her excitement. Amy hadn't ever gone anywhere, done anything, and she was taken in by him. He sickened me with all his boasting, but poor naive Amy fell for it."

"And you couldn't talk her out of it?"

"No. After all, I was about to leave for Los Angeles and college. Amy pointed out that I was following my dream, and she had the right to follow hers."

"What did they use for money?"

"Her share of the college fund my folks had set up for us, and a little life insurance policy they'd left. It wasn't that much, but it seemed to satisfy Richard. The way he acted, you'd have thought he found an heiress. Anyway, I tried to reason with Amy, but nothing I said influenced her."

"And then?"

"He took her to Las Vegas, and I went off to school. I didn't hear from her for almost a year. By that time, she was pregnant and Richard had left her on the ranch alone while he went off to con someone else. I came home on semester break, helped out where I could. Then Richard came back again and asked her to forgive him."

"What did he do, run out of money?"

"How did you guess? Amy fell for it and gave him the money she'd saved working in the drugstore in Juniper. Money she'd saved for the baby. Anyway, he promised me he'd stick around until the baby was born. Next thing I knew, Amy called to tell me she'd had twins. I couldn't leave in the middle of a semester, but I came as soon as possible. Richard was fit to be tied. He couldn't stomach twins, and, Lord knew, I couldn't stomach him! But I put up with him for Amy's sake. She loved him, no matter what he did, and he traded on that."

"You said he didn't stick around for long."

"No. He conned Amy out of the last of her money and left saying he was going to 'invest' it and make the ranch a showplace. He even told her he'd hire help to take care of the twins so she wouldn't have to work so hard." Sara laughed ruefully. "It was the last Amy heard from him. The only help Amy ever got was from Miguel, and from me. Miguel stayed to watch over the twins, and I went back to Los Angeles, got a job and sent money home."

"My poor Sam. Never did get to lead a life of your own, did you?"

"Sure I did. I had Steven, then. Things were going as well as could be expected when Amy called to tell me they'd discovered she had cancer. My job folded about then, so I came down here. Steven transferred with the company and said goodbye when he heard about the twins. Said he wasn't ready for fatherhood and being holed up in a hick town like Juniper. I guess I had no better luck than Amy in choosing a man."

"And now, you've got me hanging around. Lord knows, you deserve better than that. Come here."

She came into his arms. He helped her dry her eyes and carried her into the parlor. He sat on the couch with her in his lap and hugged her tightly. "I'm going to see to it your brother-in-law doesn't get to first base, not with the kids and not with the ranch. I don't know how, yet. But I'm not going to let him, or anyone else, hurt you, Sam."

She tried to push away from him. "Richard mustn't find us like this anymore. We've got to keep away from each other."

"Maybe I should leave the house. I hate to suggest it, but if you're going to worry what Richard might think if I stay, it's probably better if I go back to the lean-to."

"It would be best." She smiled through new tears, a wistful smile that tore at his heart. "But, I *will* remember you and our night together."

Quinn kissed her tenderly, held her against him for a moment. "Come on. If this is going to be our last night together for a while, I want to spend it with you in my arms."

"Quinn, I don't dare—"

"Dare for once, Sam. For me?"

"For me, too," she whispered against his chest. "Especially for me."

Hand in hand, they went up the stairs and into Sara's room.

Sara drank in the tender smile on Quinn's face as he took off her shirt, savored the feel of his warm hands as they brushed her shoulders. He loosened her bra, held her breasts and kissed each one until it hardened with desire. He unfastened her jeans and slid them down over her legs, kissing the inside of her thighs. Murmuring soft words of admiration, he held her away from him and gazed at her, almost if he were seeing her for the first time.

She stopped him with a kiss. "My turn," she whispered. "If this is going to be the last time we have together, I want to touch you as you touched me."

She removed the open shirt that hung from his shoulders, and gave in to the urge to rub her fingers through the soft curls on his chest. He felt every bit as good as he looked. She wanted him, needed him. "You must have been sent by my guardian angel," she murmured and held her breath when he stepped out of his jeans and his desire became all too evident. "Quinn?"

With a short laugh, he drew her to the bed. "Can't help it. You do the damnedest things to me. But, tonight, I just want to hold you in my arms. Nothing more."

As Sara curled against him and closed her eyes, Quinn marveled at the restraint he was able to maintain. At the strong, almost overwhelming feeling that made him her protector instead of her lover.

He recalled making love to her last night and the way she'd promised to remember him. As for himself, he would remember her, too.

Forever.

Chapter Nine

Now that McClintock had come home, Quinn was back to bunking in the lean-to and washing up in a hand basin with cold water. Leaving the house had been his idea, after noting Sara's nervous glances. She had enough on her hands without constantly looking over her shoulder.

Muttering his displeasure, he lathered a washcloth and washed his face and naked torso. Hell, washing this way was more like taking a spit bath, he grumbled with disgust as he dried his chest. If he stayed around the Lazy M much longer, he was going to have to rig up some kind of shower so he could wash all over at the same time. It was another grievance to chalk up against McClintock.

He eyed the narrow cots and the curtained corner that passed as a closet, cursed under his breath and continued pacing the small area; twelve steps there, twelve steps back. After sleeping in a feather bed across the hall from Sara, there was no comparison between the accommodations in the house and the lean-to. He didn't mind sharing the meager quarters with Miguel, but that wasn't what was really teeing him off.

He missed Sara, terribly.

Her tears had affected him more than he realized. He leaned against the doorway, gazed off at the house and thought about the woman he'd nicknamed "Sam." What was she doing to cope with her fears, now that he wasn't there to hold her, to reassure her? And what of the twins, how were they doing, now that they'd met their father and obviously feared him? The urge to protect the three of them was so strong, and his inability to do it so frustrating, he felt as if he were back behind the iron bars of Juniper's jailhouse.

In the night, he'd imagined her in bed, tears staining her cheeks. Waiting for McClintock to make his move, as he'd promised. As strong as she was trying to be, she was still a woman trying to protect her young, and with no man to stand by her.

He paced the floor, cursing the bad luck that kept him from her side. He should have been up at the house taking care of her and the twins, and he would have if Sara wasn't so afraid of his temper and of McClintock's dirty mind. But maybe it was better this way. For now.

He hadn't been able to come up with a way to get rid of the louse. He had to think of something, and soon. For Sara and the twins' sake.

He missed her more than he'd ever imagined possible, but it didn't look as if he was going to be able to be any closer to her than across a kitchen table any-time soon. Even then, they ate in silence, quickly glancing away when their eyes met. Her uneasiness had even communicated itself to the children. Jase had lapsed into uncharacteristic quiet, Katie clutched her teddy bear to her chest as if she were afraid someone was going to take it from her. Even Miguel looked troubled. As for Prince, the pup focused his re-proachful stare at Quinn as if Quinn were to blame for all of this silence.

As far as Quinn could see, getting rid of Mc-Clintock would be doing all of them a great favor, even the pup. His own grievance against McClintock had become personal. He couldn't stand to see the change in Sara and the kids.

When had he started thinking of them as his family?

He threw the damp towel on a chair and continued his pacing. Now that he felt strong enough, he supposed he should tell Sara he was ready to go back to work. Not that he looked forward to laboring in the punishing sun again, but at least it would be one way he and Sara could be far from McClintock's sleazy, suspicious eyes.

Once they were out of sight in the south pasture, he'd be able to take Sara in his arms again. He'd show her how much he missed her and he'd take it slow and easy. Very slow and easy. Twisting uncomfortably as his jeans grew tight, he added another notch in the score against McClintock.

But first things first. He had to find a way to get to town, locate a telephone that afforded some privacy and talk to Bill Edwards. Bill had a lot of connections. Once they'd been pretty shady, but he had straightened himself out. Quinn had learned a lot from Bill, and they had traded favors more than once.

If McClintock's behavior meant anything, the man was all bluster, but he would bear watching. From what Sara had told about him, there had to be a reason that had brought McClintock to Juniper, and it wasn't the twins. Thank God. They didn't need a good-for-nothing father like McClintock. Juniper and the Lazy M just weren't McClintock's style. There had to be a more compelling reason for him to be here. He was determined to find it. He owed Sara that much.

"Quinn?" Sara stood in the doorway.

He spun on his heel. For a moment he wasn't sure if she were real. "Sam? Is that really you or are you a figment of my imagination?" Hands outstretched in welcome, a broad smile on his face, he strode to meet her.

She held up her hand to stop him. "Please, wait a minute. I have to talk to you." When he started to draw her into the room and close the door behind her, she shook her head. "Leave the door open. You never know who's watching."

"Why, is McClintock back?"

"No, but we can't know when he'll show up. He knows the ranch pretty well. He could even be hiding somewhere."

"Let the... sorry. Let him watch." The unhappy look on her face kept him from reaching out to her. "Sam, I've missed you. I want you back in my arms where you belong."

"I miss you, too, but Richard's just looking for trouble and I can't afford to let him find it. There's no telling what he would do if he found out about us." She gazed at him with anxious eyes. "I have to get into town, to the bank. Will you keep an eye on the place?"

"The bank?"

"Yes. I'm going to see about getting a loan before Andrews gets my credit turned off."

"Why would he want to do something like that?"

"I'm not sure, but I've decided it's to force me to share the ranch with Richard, or to buy it himself. Or, maybe," she added thoughtfully, "to use it to blackmail me into giving the custody of the twins to Richard." Her frown deepened, her eyes grew angry. "Andrews is capable of doing anything."

"Hey, that day will never come, if I can help it." He ached to hold her, to comfort her. "If you're that worried about what your brother-in-law and the judge might do, maybe I'd better come with you."

Doubt filled her eyes. "I'm not looking for trouble."

"Sometimes it comes uninvited, Sam. It's better to be prepared. Let me come with you."

"Well, maybe, if you promise not to lose your temper."

"Sam, I'd never do anything to hurt you. Don't you know that by now?" He shoved his hands in his pockets to keep from pulling her into his arms. He wanted to hold her, give her part of his own strength, keep her safe.

What he was going to do was play bodyguard. And heaven help anyone who tried to hurt her.

"Maybe we can take the long way into town and talk things over," he said. "There's no crime in talking, is there?"

"No. I'd like that." She paused for a moment before her face lighted up. "There's a small pond in a grove of trees a few miles out of town—sort of like an oasis. As far as I know, Richard's never been there. In fact, no one ever goes there at this time of the year. I'll pack a lunch and we'll stop for a quick picnic."

She eyed his chest and blushed. "Better put on a shirt. You shouldn't be exposed to the sun so soon after you almost had sunstroke."

"Sam, you sure have this thing about shirts. Care to explain?"

She blushed again. "Hurry up. We can't stay away for long. I don't trust Richard. I have a feeling he's involved in something unpleasant, and I don't want him coming around when I'm not here."

"Okay. You were saying?"

"I said I know of a place where we can be alone."

"Sam, I knew you were an angel. Come on, let's get going. It's been pure torture having you so close and untouchable."

"I know, I feel the same way." She glanced behind her. "I can't leave the twins here alone for long. They're frightened enough as it is. I've asked Miguel to keep an eye on them. He's going to take them up the hill on a treasure hunt." A shy smile curved at her lips. "Jase is determined to find a pot of gold to give to you."

"To me?"

"Yes. He figures if he finds enough gold, you'll stay."

The yearning in her eyes gave her away. It looked as if Jase wasn't the only one who wanted to keep him here.

"Sam, I'm not going to make any promises I can't keep. Judge Andrews was pretty clear that he intended to see me run out of town. I don't know if I'll be allowed to stay after my sentence is over, even if I want to."

"I know." Her saddened coffee-colored eyes met his own. "It's just that Jase is afraid his father is going to decide to come back to the ranch to stay. I can't seem to make him believe I'd never allow that. Richard is no shining example of fatherhood. Poor little man. Jase said he'd rather have you for a father."

She was right about the twins' father. As far as Quinn was concerned, he wouldn't even trust Spike the mule to a man like Richard McClintock, let alone a child. As for himself being a father to Jase and Katie, Quinn hadn't ever thought about having children. But if he did, he wouldn't mind having a son and a daughter like them. Someday.

"The children are something else. As for Jase, he's a wise old man in a kid's body. Does he ever stop thinking, take time to be a little boy?"

"No. Right now, he thinks finding the gold for you is the answer to his problem."

"I've already found my gold, Sam."

The soft look in his eyes held her mesmerized. "You have? Where?"

"When I looked through the jailhouse bars and caught a glimpse of you passing by. Your hair was shining like spun gold in the sunlight. It almost blinded me. I wanted to touch it then. I want to touch it now."

He ached to run his fingers through her hair. He wanted to pull her into his arms and slam the door shut on McClintock and the rest of the world, but the way she kept looking over her shoulder kept him at arm's length. She had enough trouble without him causing her any more.

His self-control was near to breaking. The longing in Sara's voice matched his own. Remembering their night together made his body throb. "I need to hold you in my arms, Sam. To make you feel safe and wanted."

When she voiced a low sound of pleasure, ripples of warmth ran through him, igniting desire along the way.

"THERE'S THE CUTOFF." Sara pointed to a narrow county road that led off the highway. "We'll follow that road for about three-quarters of a mile. The oasis is over there, under the trees."

They drove through a grove of pine and sycamore trees, across dry and dusty fire trails and into a small meadow. There, in the midst of dry grass and parched earth, was a small pond. A thirsty deer darted away at their arrival. A trio of squirrels, sitting on a tree limb that had fallen across the shallow water, rose on their hind legs and scolded the new arrivals.

Quinn waved to the noisy trio. "Take a break, fellows. We won't be staying long." Not long enough to suit him, anyway. But he was ready to settle for whatever time they had. He took the picnic basket out of the truck and checked out their surroundings. "This is an oasis? It looks more like a half-dry water hole."

"You have to pretend," Sara answered with a happy smile. "I do it all the time."

Quinn was lost in her smile. When her eyes sparkled like they did now, she didn't look much older than the twins. He was willing to believe her world was part make-believe, since pretending was probably the only way she could have made it through the past few years. He was so tickled with the change in her, he wanted to hug her, pick her up in his arms and twirl her against the bright blue sky. And when he let her down, he'd let her slide slowly down his body, reacquainting himself with every one of her soft curves.

"Sam?" Quinn's voice was low and inviting.

Shivers ran through Sara. As much as she wanted to throw herself into his arms, she hesitated. Although she'd agreed to the tryst, she hesitated. After all, they were out in the open where any eyes could find them.

"There's just not much water around this time of year," she said, nervously putting words between them. "When there is, I bring the kids here to go swimming. Not that it's ever real deep, but the kids don't seem to mind. They like to pretend it's a lake."

Quinn sighed. His lady was shy. Nice, in a way. He wouldn't rush her.

"Pretending runs in the family, doesn't it?" he asked with compassion. Pretending. Just the thought made him feel younger and more carefree than he'd been in a long while. That was probably how they'd all been able to get through death and hardship. No, he thought with a flash of insight, their strength was in having each other. No matter how hard things were, they had each other to depend on. Lucky kids, lucky aunt.

"Does the water ever get deep enough to swim?"

"Sometimes." Sara motioned to the squirrels. "I suppose they wouldn't be here if there wasn't water."

"Water or not, the squirrels are doing what comes naturally," Quinn replied. He wanted to do what came naturally to him, too: take her in his arms and make love to her under the cloudless blue sky. To make love to her until her eyes took on that special look that never failed to send desire shooting through him. And he'd waited long enough.

"Okay, Sam. Now that we're in a desert oasis, let's take advantage of it."

He spread the light blanket between them, knelt down and pulled Sara into his arms. "Now, this is what I call a real picnic," he whispered as his lips brushed her forehead, her eyelids, her cheeks.

As she returned his kisses, the worry lines disappeared from her forehead. A deep sigh escaped her as she melted against him and closed her eyes. "This is wonderful."

"Good. There's no one here but you and me. Now relax and enjoy yourself. You're with me now, safe. I'd never let Richard or anyone else hurt you."

"The squirrels are watching," she whispered when his hand toyed with the buttons on her blouse.

Sure enough, three sets of mud brown eyes regarded them steadily from the tree limb. A family of bluebirds chattered. A lone deer peeked around a bush and bounded away again.

He looked over his shoulder at the watching birds and animals. "I'm willing to bet that they'll never tell. But if they worry you, ignore them and they'll go away." Quinn spoke softly as he set himself to unbuttoning her blouse. He bent to his task, kissing every inch of her golden flesh as it was exposed to his gaze. "Mmm. You taste so good."

"Hungry? I made cheese sandwiches."

"There's all kinds of hunger, Sam. Right now, I'm hungry for you." Playfully he nipped at her chin. The yearning that sprang into her eyes drove his laughter away. He held her in his arms, pressed her against his chest. Her hair hung down to her shoulders in golden disarray. He smoothed it away from her face with a gentle hand. "I meant what I said before, Sam. One night with you wasn't enough. I want you now and I'll want you for all the tomorrows we have together. I'm not even sure I'll ever be ready to let you go."

"All the tomorrows we have together," she echoed. So it wasn't only Richard McClintock that would keep them apart, she thought sadly. He was still a drifter with restless feet. Was he telling her there was no future for them beyond these few days?

Quinn sensed her unease. "Don't think about tomorrow, Sam. We have today."

"One day isn't enough for me," she whispered.

"Not for me, either. So what are we going to do about it?"

"I don't know." She moved out of his arms. "Maybe planning this picnic wasn't such a good idea, after all. I might get used to it, and then what will I do when you're gone?"

"Come here, Sam."

"Why? You *are* going to leave soon, aren't you?"

"I said, come here."

When she drifted back into his arms, he cradled her head under his chin and caressed her tenderly. "I can't promise how many more times there'll be, Sam. But I will promise you I'll try."

Silence fell between them as he drew her blouse from her shoulders and kissed the soft swell of each breast. At her sharp intake of breath, a pleased smile curved at his lips. "Let me love you, Sam," he whispered as he kissed his way up her throat to her lips. "Let me love you."

Silently Sara closed her eyes.

"What's wrong, Sam?" He raised his head. "I thought you wanted this as much as I did."

"I do, but I can't help thinking how few days there are left before you leave."

"Don't think. The days on a calendar are only numbers."

He was wrong. Days on a calendar were real, too real. Now that she'd found Quinn, the days rushed by as though driven by a Santa Ana wind, a wind that threatened her even as she was pulled into a whirlpool of sensuality. Was that to be her future? Ten days of stolen pleasure, and then only memories?

She knew it was more than physical infatuation and desire she felt for Quinn. He excited her, tantalized her, made her dream of love even while she wasn't certain love was what they shared. He exuded strength, made her feel whole, safe. He was the type of man a woman needed in her life. Her mind and her awakened senses clamored for more of him, all of him.

She gazed into his questioning eyes. Suddenly she wasn't strong enough to turn him away. She didn't want to, couldn't bear to. Better not to think about tomorrow before the dream was spoiled.

She let her senses take over, drowning in the sound of his voice as he whispered love words in her ear. She drank in the taste of him as he kissed her, and surrendered willingly to his searching hands. His fingers brushed her skin and wrought magic as they played across her body. He was playing her as if he were playing a violin, and the music she heard tugged at her heartstrings. Her breath caught in her throat as his handsome face and strong, heated body leaned over her. For now, he was hers. It would have to be enough.

Without words, she undid Quinn's shirt, drew it from him as she stroked his chest and covered him with quick kisses. As if drawn to a magnet, the soft hair curled around her fingers, caressing her as surely as Quinn's lips had caressed her breasts. Desperate to have him fill her, to soothe away the burning desire she felt, she reached for his belt and struggled to undo the buckle. "There's something about your belt buckle...I can never undo it."

He eyed her playfully. "You'll have to practice more often. Here. For now, I'll be happy to oblige. But only if you let me return the favor."

Her eyebrows rose in mock indignation as she joined him in making a game of the situation. "And who are you to take such liberties, sir?"

"The man who discovered that enchanting dimple on your captivating—"

Laughing, Sara covered his lips with her hand. "No need to be so explicit. However, if you'd like to pursue your investigations?"

"Most definitely, madam. Allow me." He unzipped her jeans and slowly drew them down her slender but lush hips.

"Ah, I do believe I've found something else of interest."

"And what is that, sir?"

"A tiny mole on your left hip." He bent to kiss it. "Upon further thought, I find there are other areas of interest that require my investigation."

"You lovable fool." Before she opened her arms wide and offered herself to him, Sara stirred herself to ask. "What about lunch?"

"Leave it to the squirrels."

He made love to her slowly, with his lips, his fingertips, his whole body. She was on fire with the need to become one with him, to have her whole being arch in overwhelming sensation before it exploded into a colorful burst of flame.

He brought her again and again to the edge of ecstasy, then retreated to make other discoveries that aroused her as never before. She touched him in wild passion, urged him to her. He laughed softly under his breath and joined his body to her. "Come with me, Sam," he whispered against her lips.

It was a golden day, a golden time, Sara thought, as his love brought her to a golden climax.

Content, replete with loving, she knew she'd never been so happy. Quinn meant so much to her. He calmed her fears and renewed her strength. She leaned her head against his shoulder, drinking in the masculine scent of him before she moved out of his arms. He was a wonderful, good man, but could he live in her world? Did he even intend to try?

WHILE SARA WENT into the bank, Quinn headed for the drugstore and its telephone. The pharmacy was empty, the telephone in a corner at the rear. Glancing around him to make sure he was alone, Quinn called Bill Edwards. Collect.

"Bill, it's Quinn. Got a favor to ask of you." He described Richard McClintock and his unexpected return. "After seeing the guy, I can't figure out what he wants around here. He's not the rancher type, and he sure isn't cut out to be a father, either."

"Maybe your warden has plenty of money. A slug like her brother-in-law sounds like he has a nose for it."

"No. She's dirt poor. The kids don't have any money, either."

"Maybe he wants the ranch for a front, to run drugs. You're close to the border, aren't you?"

"Could be. If so, he has it made. His cousin, Judge Andrews, is the local law. Somehow, I think he's involved in whatever McClintock is up to. With guys like that, it's got to be more than blood ties that they have in common."

"Hey, having the law covering for you is heaven for a drug dealer. Could have used a setup like that for myself, once."

"Come on, Bill. Just find out if there's any scuttlebutt on the street about McClintock and Judge Lester Andrews. But watch yourself. I wouldn't want you to get hurt. And don't mention Sara's name, for Pete's sake. If it turns out to be drugs, the last thing she needs is anyone nosing around here."

"I'll spread the word, quietlike. In the meantime, watch yourself, buddy. Guys like that like to play rough."

"I'm not worried about myself. It's Sara and the kids I'm worried about. I'll call again soon."

Quinn hung up. When he turned, the druggist was watching him from across the prescription counter.

Quinn's heart missed a beat as he met the man's thoughtful gaze. The man had probably heard every word he'd said. What had he said about drugs? Nothing really. Bill had said what was necessary and he'd only responded.

"You the fellow that got himself arrested and farmed out to Sara Martin?"

"Yes, sir." Quinn was in no mood to trade insults with the locals. One vacation in Juniper's jailhouse was enough.

"Glad you did, although I don't suppose you share my feelings." The tall, lean druggist folded his arms across his chest and waited for Quinn's answer.

Quinn didn't want to discuss his brush with the law, but the man seemed decent enough. "Working for Ms. Martin hasn't been all that bad."

The druggist nodded. He came around the counter and sized up Quinn. "I remember Sara and her younger sister, Amy, when they were kids. The Martins were good folks. Too bad they were killed in that auto crash." He paused for effect. "Things might have been different if they'd been alive."

"You don't say." Quinn was interested, but he didn't want to appear to be too eager. Small towns were big on privacy. The fact that the druggist had opened up must have meant Quinn had passed some kind of test in the man's mind. He must want him to help Sara. That was okay with Quinn. It was going to be his chance to hear Sara's story from someone who obviously was fond of her.

"Sara took off for the big city. I heard that she did right well for herself." He shook his head. "Not Amy, though. Richard McClintock showed up, fed her a line and worked her good. He was going to strike it rich, show her the bright city lights, how to have fun. Whatever he showed her, it didn't last long. They came back to the Martin place when Amy was six months pregnant. After she gave birth to twins, I never did see an angrier man. You'd have thought that Amy had committed a crime, having two kids instead of one. He took off soon after. That was, let me think, about four years ago. Never did see him again until the other day when I saw him coming out of Lester Andrews's place. They're cousins, you know."

Quinn nodded. "And Amy?"

"She kept going for a few years, but I could see it wasn't easy. Sara tried to help, too, but Amy didn't let on how bad things were, not until she had to."

The druggist glanced back at the shelves of pharmaceuticals and shrugged. "I tried to give Amy a hand with medicine and such, but she was too proud to take it. Said she'd gotten herself into the mess and she'd handle it her way. Poor soul struggled along until she found out how sick she was. That's when she asked Sara to come back to the ranch. Not for herself, you understand. It was for the kids' sake."

"Isn't Judge Andrews family?"

"Lester Andrews wasn't a help, either, until Sheriff Cable brought you in. That must have been when he thought of the work-furlough sentence." The druggist snorted his disgust. "It was a way he could help Sara without spending a dime of his own."

"Strange that he would pick now to do it. What kind of a guy is the judge?"

"Stays inside of the law, I guess. But he levies the highest fines in the county, from what I hear. Money hungry as all get-out."

"You vote for him?"

"Hell, no. Much good it did me. He's got most of the town in his pocket, one way or another. Except me and Sara."

"You and Sara," Quinn echoed. "No wonder she feels so much alone."

"Well, young man. It sounds as if Sara's got you now. I expect you'll treat her like the lady she is?"

Quinn agreed. The druggist held out his hand. "Name's Thomas Bregman. Call me Tom. Let me know if I can be of help to Sara. Not everyone around here has the same stripe down his back as Cable and Lester Andrews."

Quinn shook his hand. "Sara's lucky to have a friend like you, Tom. I'm glad to know she won't be alone."

The druggist pulled on his chin. "That's right," he said with emphasis. "You leaving as soon as your sentence is up."

"I hadn't thought about it much, until recently." Quinn hesitated and shook his head. "I tend to let tomorrow take care of itself."

Bregman shot him a quizzical glance. He gestured toward the phone. "Don't say? From what I heard, it 'pears to me you've taken quite an interest in our Sara."

Quinn exchanged a resolute glance with Bregman. The man's thoughtful gaze reflected a question that Quinn felt compelled to answer. As he turned to leave the drugstore, he looked back over his shoulder. "For what it's worth, Tom, before I go I'm going to get those worry lines off Sara Ann Martin's forehead. One way or another."

Chapter Ten

He met up with Sara as she was coming out of the bank. From the dejected expression on her face, things didn't look good.

"Any luck?"

"No. Andrews got there before me. He's persuaded Jenkins that title to the ranch is going to be contested by my brother-in-law and that it wouldn't be wise to lend any money Jenkins might never see again."

"I thought your sister willed her share to the kids?" He fell into step beside her. "What makes him think he can get a piece of it now?"

"She did, but Jenkins was told Richard is going to court to claim a widower's share."

"Would it do him any good?"

"I doubt it, since my parents left the ranch to Amy and myself. As far as I know, Amy was smart enough not to change title even though she gave him all the money she had. But he can make things very uncomfortable for a while."

She shook her hair away from her eyes and gazed around her. "Almost everyone in town owes Andrews for something or other. I tried to reason with Jenkins, but he doesn't want to get involved. Under the circumstances, I can't say that I blame him."

"Where does that leave you and the kids?"

"Back to square one—boarding horses. The money you gave me will buy enough feed for a month or two. All I need now are horses to board," she said bitterly, "and the way it looks, there aren't any."

Quinn took her by the arm and guided her to the weather-beaten truck. "Get in. Maybe we can think of something on the way home."

Home. When had he started thinking of the Lazy M as home?

"Like?"

"As much as I hate to suggest it, you could sell out and go back to L.A."

"Never! I promised Amy I'd keep the ranch for the kids. Hell will freeze over before I let their father get his hands on it." In spite of his advice to Sara, Quinn wasn't planning on giving up, either. Not when he'd finally found a place where he felt he belonged, and when Sara and the children were part of it.

She was fighting for her family like a lioness for her cubs. He shared the feeling.

The score against McClintock was growing every day. The creep was going to get what he deserved, but quietly. He didn't want to shake up Sara and the kids;

he had to get McClintock to leave under his own
steam.

He swung into the cab and put his hand over hers.
"You're not alone in this, Sam. I want to help you."

At the grateful look she gave him, he yearned to
gather her in his arms and kiss the worry lines on her
forehead away.

"Thanks, but it's not your problem. I'll take care of
Richard."

*Just like you take care of everything and everyone
else. But who's going to take care of you?*

Quinn brooded over Sara's bad luck. How could
anyone so caring and giving be in so much trouble? he
wondered. She needed someone on her side. For a
change, someone who didn't want anything from her.
He was going to be the one, no matter what she said.
It was just going to be a matter of time.

They drove by the cutoff to the oasis where he and
Sara had stopped on their way into town. Had it been
only a short time ago that Sara had been so happy, so
hopeful? And so loving?

His body quickened when he recalled her silken skin
against his, the way her breath had caught when he
caressed her body. Her soft words of pleasure had
loosened the flood of desire he had been trying to
control. They'd come together with a need so great
that the sensual explosion had left them both breathless.

Touch for touch, kiss for kiss, taste for taste, as if
she was afraid it would be the last time they would

have together, she'd returned his passion with wild abandon.

But it wasn't going to be the last time. Not if he had anything to say about it.

A faint pink tinged Sara's face. He took her hand in his and smiled in the sure knowledge that she was remembering their "picnic," too.

He tried to perk up her spirits. "I wonder if the squirrels and the birds enjoyed the sandwiches we left them."

"I'm sure." She laughed weakly. The flush deepened when she glanced over at him. "You missed a great sandwich. I put in extra cheese."

"Lucky squirrels. As for me, I don't feel I missed a thing. How about you?"

A soft smile was his answer. He gently squeezed her hand in silent communication. "Maybe we can picnic more often."

"I'd like that," she answered, a wistful smile on her lips, "but the chances aren't too good. We have to keep a low profile or someone could decide I'm not a fit guardian for the twins."

"They don't come any better. We'll find the time, Sam. You mean a lot to me." He was surprised at the depth of his response to this woman. He couldn't remember ever feeling this way before.

"You mean a lot to me and the children, too, Quinn. I'm grateful for your friendship and the way you are with the twins. They sure are taken with you."

"Thanks. That's good to know. It hasn't been difficult to be nice to them." *And you, too,* he wanted to add. But now was not the time to get serious about anyone, not until he was a free man and had solved her problems. And his own.

He'd spent most of his adult life running, insisting on his freedom. To give it up, to fall in love, even with someone like Sara didn't come easy.

But he was beginning to believe he could.

The realization that tomorrow might be too late to tell her how he felt made him uneasy. With the way things were going, who knew what tomorrow might bring?

"Sam, don't give up too soon. I have a feeling that things are going to change."

"Unless you have a money tree, or Jase finds that pot of gold, I don't see how."

Jase and Katie were waiting for them by the open gate when they reached home. Smiling, Sara pulled to a stop.

"Look what Jase found, Aunt Sara!"

"Another dog?" Quinn opened the cab door and let the twins squeeze in between Sara and him. Jase held a small bottle in his hand. Tiny pieces of fool's gold nestled in the bottom.

"Is this enough, Mr. Tucker?"

"Enough for what?" Quinn wanted to know.

Jase looked up at him with earnest eyes. "To pay you to stay with us forever and ever."

Quinn was taken aback. "I don't want money, Jase. You know I was only supposed to stay with you and your aunt for a short time. That time will be up soon and I may have to leave."

His eyes narrowed when he recalled Judge Andrews had told him to get out of Juniper when his sentence was over, but he couldn't tell that to Jase. "I have important things to do."

"Like my Dad?"

Quinn froze. He met Sara's stricken eyes over the top of Jase's head. He put his arm around the boy and ruffled his hair. "Never! I'm not like your dad!"

"Then you're going to stay with us?"

Sara choked back a comment.

"Let's take it one day at a time, shall we?" Quinn nuzzled tangled blond hair. "We'll worry about tomorrow when it gets here."

Jase and Katie exchanged troubled glances. "Maybe we should go find more gold," Katie whispered. "Maybe we don't have enough."

Quinn was shocked. He'd thought Sara was just joking when she mentioned the twins were looking for gold. "It's not the money!"

"Does that mean you're going to leave?" Jase persisted.

Sara broke in before Quinn could answer. "Go and play, now, children. I'll have dinner ready soon. Tonight we're having something you're really going to like."

Obediently the dejected children slid down from the truck and trudged up the dirt road to the house. Quinn grew even more troubled when he saw Jase put his arm around his sister's small shoulders and whisper in her ear as they disappeared from sight.

"Sam, I never..." The motor drowned him out.

Sara drove the short distance to the barn, stopped the truck and turned to face him. "It's not your fault. I should have seen it coming. I shouldn't have allowed this to happen. They've lost their father and now they're going to lose you. I should never have brought you here." Tears gathered in her eyes.

He should have realized how needy the children were for a man in their lives, that his interest in them might lead them to think he was something more than a man who was just passing through their lives.

He wanted to draw Sara into his arms, soothe away her tears. Tell her that he'd started the ball rolling to settle the score with McClintock. But what if it didn't work out? She didn't need any more heartache. She already had enough to last her a lifetime.

"Sam, honestly, I'm sorry. I never meant to have the twins become so attached to me. The last thing I intended was for the children to think of me as a father figure, especially since I never had a real father of my own. It just seemed to happen." He shook his head in bewilderment. "I've never been around kids before. For that matter, I'm not even sure I was ever a kid myself. Not the way I was brought up, farmed out from relative to relative and in foster homes where

they didn't let you be a child. I didn't dream things
would turn out this way."

"The twins are so vulnerable," she whispered.
"Especially now that their father's back in the picture." She looked at him with stricken eyes. "Children are drawn to a strong protector. I guess they
figured you could take care of them."

He sat there, unable to move or speak. In spite of
his good intentions, he was the cause of another
heartbreak for Sara, Jase and Katie. He didn't know
what to say.

"Well, you've been gone long enough," a sour voice
broke in. "Are you gonna sit there all day, or are you
going to come out and talk?"

Sara shot out of the cab. "What are you doing
here?"

"Just dropped in to see the kids, but they ran away
when I drove up. I have the right to see them, you
know."

"Who says so?"

"My cousin Lester, that's who."

"Not on your life! You've caused them enough un-
happiness."

Sara looked ready to fight.

"No, let me take care of this." Quinn stayed her
hand. "You go on in to the kids." He waited until she
reluctantly started toward the house, then squared off
with a smirking McClintock. "I thought Sara made it
clear you're not welcome here. Get the hell out of here

and don't come back before you lose those pearly white teeth of yours."

"So that's the way it is! You're not just a hired hand. You and Sara are—" McClintock swallowed his words when Quinn took a menacing step toward him. "You're nothing but a jailbird, a bought hand. You can't tell me what to do on my own property!"

"It's not your property, and I just did. Now, get the hell out of here!"

McClintock glared at Sara's disappearing figure, shuffled his feet while he tried to think of a rejoinder, then rushed for his car when Quinn raised a clenched fist.

DINNER WAS QUIETER than usual. The twins picked at their food and stole glances at Quinn when they thought he wasn't looking.

"I thought you two liked ham," Sara said with a worried frown on her face.

The twins shrugged.

"How about some candied sweet potatoes?"

The twins shook their heads.

"Asparagus?"

The twins made a face.

Quinn put down his fork. "Go on outside and play, Jase, Katie. You can eat later if you get hungry."

He waited until the twins left the kitchen, shrugged his shoulders and pushed his own plate away. "You can save my dinner, too. I'm going to go out and talk to the kids. If you need me, I'll be out back."

Outside, Quinn could hear the twins whispering and moving around in their tree house. Not that he knew much about the way four-year-old children think, but their secrecy told him that they were up to something. "Jase! Katie! Come on down here!"

Twin blond heads looked out the small window.

"I said, come on down here."

Quinn silently watched the play of emotions pass over their faces as they climbed down the narrow ladder and ended up in front of him. "Got something on your minds?"

Katie brought her clenched hands to her breast.

Jase squared his shoulders, swallowed hard, opened his mouth to speak and promptly closed it.

"Not talking, eh?"

"No sir," Jase managed bravely. "It's our secret."

It was no use. He'd never solve anything by frightening them. "Look, guys. If you've got something on your mind, let me in on it. Maybe I can help."

The twins waited, their stares unwavering. Quinn was no longer surprised to realize how much he did care about the twins, and for their aunt, for that matter. He would have had to be made of stone not to respond to the children's winning ways and Sara's loving, compassionate nature.

"Whatever the two of you are planning, forget it. Let me tell you something." He hunkered down to their eye level. "I care about you. Very much. I know I told you I couldn't hang around here much longer, but that doesn't mean I won't try to make everything okay for you and your aunt before I leave. And it doesn't mean I won't be back to visit you. Can we be friends?''

Katie reached for Jase's hand. They gazed up at him in childish defiance. His heart ached for the way they must feel; at the mercy of fighting grown-ups, with no way to protect themselves. He'd been in that situation more than once and remembered the helpless feeling.

''Well, how about it?''

The twins exchanged silent communication, then gazed back at Quinn. Katie looked unhappy, Jase resigned. If they'd decided to be friends, it was because they probably felt they had no choice.

Jase, the spokesman, finally nodded. ''Yes sir. We'll be friends with you, if you want us to. But we really want you to be our dad.''

''I wish I could be. Tell you what, let's be friends for now. Will you shake on it?''

Katie reluctantly put her hand in his. The feel of her small hand made Quinn feel as if he were Jack, the Giant Killer. Jase offered a manly handshake that nearly undid Quinn. A fierce, protective feeling for the children swept over him. Kids this age should never have to feel so vulnerable.

''Then, it's a deal. Trust me?'' He was rewarded by tentative smiles.

''Good. I promise you won't regret it.'' He hugged Katie and threw his free arm around Jase. ''Remember, now, I'm a friend of yours. You can tell me anything.''

Their brave smiles darn near broke Quinn's heart.

"Okay, go on now," he said giving them a gentle push. "And don't forget to eat something. Your aunt will be worried if you don't."

He watched them go. He might not be their father, but he was beginning to think he couldn't have loved them more than if he had been.

THE KNOWLEDGE that time was running out for Sara sent Quinn back to the south pasture to finish the fencing. The hard thrusts with the posthole digger vented his frustration and gave him time to take a good look at himself.

He'd been too young to accept the fact that his grandmother might die, leaving him alone. Bitter, angry, when she had, he'd resented the relatives who'd halfheartedly taken him in. He'd been shifted from home to home, year after year. Tired of never becoming part of any family, of never staying in one place long enough to make friends, he'd decided to make it on his own.

Young enough, and angry enough, he'd been impressed by the easy money floating around—if a guy didn't mind living on the edge of the law. Before long, he'd found himself delivering "packages," the contents of which he only suspected. All he had to show for those empty years, was a criminal record and a life of drifting.

He was thirty years old, with no family or home and few possessions. Since he'd sold his truck to repay Sara, he didn't even own transportation.

Drifting from place to place, job to job, day to day, no longer held any appeal for him.

What did appeal to him was Sara and the twins. They represented everything he'd missed in his life, and everything he now knew he wanted.

He needed them as much as they needed him.

Straightening, he held his aching ribs and counted the number of poles he still had to set in place. Stepping backward to size up the situation, he tripped when his heel caught the protruding corner of a round, wooden cover imbedded in the dry soil. Curiosity aroused, he used the metal edge of the digger and pried off the cover. He knelt and peered into the dark hole.

Quinn knew enough to recognize a dry well when he saw it. In fact, now that he thought about it, he'd noticed several of these covers on the ranch that must have been dug years ago before water was piped into the area.

He poked the posthole digger into the darkness. As he withdrew the handle, he noticed a black ripple of movement against the glare of the sun. A thick, dirty mass was dripping from the end of the pole. Puzzled, he thrust it back into the darkness as far as he could and checked it again. More of the same black mess dripped down and formed a small pool at his feet, growing larger and larger before it trickled downhill. He fingered the thick liquid, rubbed it between his fingers and sniffed. The smell was enough to raise the hairs on the back of his neck.

Oil! He'd worked in the oil fields in Bakersfield often enough to recognize it when he saw it, too. How much of it there was beneath his feet or whether it was of a high quality he didn't know, but it damn sure was oil.

He wiped his hand in the dry grass, replaced the wooden cover on the dry well, rose to his feet and pondered his discovery.

The answer to Sara's financial problems lay at his feet. So why wasn't he any happier? It didn't take a genius to figure out why. If Richard McClintock heard about the oil discovery, Sara and the twins would never get rid of the bloodsucker.

He'd have to keep his find a secret for now.

TRUCE OR NO TRUCE, friends or no, the twins still gave him the silent treatment.

Quinn watched them over the rim of his coffee cup. He wasn't feeling very talkative, either. Not only did he have a bigger problem to resolve, he knew it was going to take more than a handshake for Jase and Katie's good humor to be restored. He would have to get rid of their father. Somehow, he had to put the smiles back on their faces.

Every time he glanced at Sara, he felt like a heel. Who was he to hide the means to solve her financial problems? he asked himself. The fact that he'd decided he wanted to be more than her ''hired'' hand wouldn't cut any ice with her if she knew about the oil. Or that he was only trying to protect her from the likes of McClintock and Andrews. She was always talking about being able to take care of herself, but he was sure this was one time she'd be on the losing end of the argument.

He glanced at her work-roughened hands, the cuts that were still healing, the broken nails. Building fences wasn't easy, especially for a woman, determined though she might be. Added to that were caring for the twins, the house, the cooking, the cleaning. How she managed sure beat the hell out of him.

He fought off the impulse to tell her about the oil. He told himself it was premature to reveal its existence. No use raising her hopes—it might just be a fluke, and not worth much, anyway.

WHEN QUINN CAME into the house for breakfast the next morning, there was a note on the kitchen table from Sara telling him that she and the children had gone to the south pasture to check on the new fences.

Cold sweat broke over him. A bitter premonition turned his blood to liquid ice. He didn't know precisely why, but his sixth sense was quivering like a harp string plucked by unseen, evil fingers. It had never failed him before. Time had run out. Big trouble, bigger than he'd ever faced, was just around the corner and headed his way. He could feel it cover him like a dark cloud, so real, he could taste it. He poured himself a cup of black coffee, raided the cookie jar and went outside to sit on the front steps to wait.

SARA SURVEYED the area still to be fenced. She would only need another few days, then she'd be in business. If Quinn hadn't come down with heat exposure, the fencing would have been in by now and she could have boarded horses without having to worry about their running away. She considered the wisdom of keeping horses in the meadow without fences. It was no use. Horses instinctively knew they were meant to run free. Even if she was lucky enough to find any takers with the fence incomplete, the horses would have to be tethered. No horse owner would appreciate that.

She watched the children chase each other across the meadow. Their happy shouts warmed her heart and broke into her despondency. Thank goodness for the children; they were life's saving grace.

She ran after them. "Wait up! Jase! Katie! Wait for me!"

Laughing, they ran faster. She redoubled her efforts.

Katie tripped. Jase skidded to a stop and ran back to help her. They were no more than a few feet from a capped dry well when Sara reached them. Sinking to her knees, she caught them to her. "I guess I'm out of shape," she said trying to catch her breath. "Let's call it a tie."

"We would of won the race, Aunt Sara, but I fell."
Katie bravely showed off her skinned knee.

"Of course you would, sweetheart, but I wasn't really trying to race with you." Sara brushed pieces of grass from Katie's knee. "You're a brave girl."

"Than why did you want us to stop?"

"Because...because." Sara took a deep breath. She hated to frighten the children, but they needed to know when danger was close. She pointed to the capped well a few feet away. "That's a dry water hole over there. When I was a little girl, my father drilled for water, but there wasn't any and he had to look somewhere else. I was afraid it wasn't covered. I didn't want you to get hurt."

Curious, Jase sank back on his haunches and eyed the capped well cover. "What's this stuff, Aunt Sara?"

Sara leaned forward to examine the stiff, black ooze on the dry grass. "I don't know." She poked her finger into the mess, rubbed it between her fingers, and sniffed the substance. It was definitely oil, and it didn't look like the kind the mechanic had used when he'd lubed and oiled her car.

"What is it, Aunt Sara?" Jase repeated.

"I'm not sure, but it reminds me of an old saying: 'If it looks like oil, smells like oil and feels like oil, it's oil.' Maybe it came from the truck."

As she spoke, Sara realized the truck couldn't have been this close to the fence line, and as far as she knew, it wasn't leaking oil.

She remembered Quinn's odd behavior last night, and the calculating glances he'd given her. At the time, she hadn't thought much about it, but now she was afraid it had been more than that.

He knew about the oil! A cold wave of anger swept over her. After all she and Quinn had come to mean to each other, how could he still have hidden something so important from her? How could she have made love with a man who'd cared so little for her that he'd betrayed her? And after he'd told her how much he wanted to care for and protect her and the twins! She felt besmirched by his touch, his kisses, his lies.

THE MINUTE QUINN SPOTTED the truck speeding down the dirt road, he knew he was too late. He didn't know how, but somehow Sara had stumbled on to his discovery. He sighed, rose to his feet and walked down to meet the truck.

"Sara?"

She pushed past him and went into the house. His heart constricted at the set expression on her face. Before he could follow her, she was back. She showed him her smudged fingers.

"Did you find oil in the south pasture?"

"Well, yes, I did," he said reluctantly. He couldn't lie to her, no matter the consequences. When she turned white, he hurried to add, "I had a reason for not telling you."

"Even when you knew how much I needed a financial windfall? How could you?"

Confronted with an anguished Sara, Quinn's reasons for keeping the truth from her no longer seemed important. "I can explain."

"Were you planning to get something out of this for yourself?"

"Good Lord, no! It never entered my mind."

"Take this." She thrust at Quinn the money he had given her to buy his freedom.

"Sam, believe me, I wasn't going to hide the oil from you."

"Don't call me Sam!"

He brushed aside the money and tried to grab her hands. She pushed his away, a mixture of anger and despair on her face. In a voice breaking with emotion, she warned, "Don't you ever touch me again." At the sound of a sob, she glanced over to where a frightened Jase held Katie's hand protectively in his.

"Go on in the house, children. I'll be there in a minute. I haven't finished talking to Mr. Tucker."

Quinn's heart sank. If he was back to being Mr. Tucker, Sara was in no mood to listen to reason. He had the sinking feeling that no amount of explaining was going to reach her.

Sara waited until the twins had wandered away before she swung back to face Quinn. "How could you hide the answer to my prayers, when you've made love to me and told me how much you care about me and the twins?"

Quinn didn't want to believe this was happening. Not after all they had meant to each other. "What does my finding oil have to do with it, Sa . . . Sara. I made love to you because we both wanted it."

"That was purely physical on your part, and stupidity on mine. You were so good at sweet-talking that I believed you cared for me."

"I do care for you. I never intended to hurt you. Be honest with yourself. You wanted me, too."

"That's right," she admitted, "but now I know it was nothing more than lust." She covered her eyes with a trembling hand. "I thought you were different, but you're no better than Steven or Richard. I should have known all you men are alike. You find a woman's weakness and then you prey on it."

Quinn felt as if he'd been hit in his gut by a giant fist. He'd never felt so rotten in his life. He was guilty of being stupid, but the knowledge that Sara thought he'd deliberately used her was more than he could handle.

"That's a low blow, Sara. I've never used a woman in my life, and I didn't use you. How can you compare me with that scum of a brother-in-law of yours?"

The wave of her hand as she dismissed the question spoke louder then words. "As if that wasn't enough, you charmed the children into believing in you. You made them care about you, trust you, led them to believe you would protect them from their father." Anguished tears rose in her eyes. "I'll get over you, but what about the children?"

Quinn's heart constricted. The children knew about the oil, had heard their aunt's questions and accusations. He'd promised them his friendship, but sure as hell they weren't thinking of him as a friend right now.

"I never lied about the way I felt about you, Sara. Nor have I ever lied to Jase and Katie. I do care for them. I care for you."

"Sure you do. As much as you're capable of caring, and it doesn't look like that's worth much," she answered bitterly. "As far as I could tell, you care for us about as much as Richard does."

"Don't you *ever* compare me to him! You can't possibly believe that. Whatever else I may have done, I've never hurt or used anyone in my life!"

She closed her eyes, drew a deep breath. "That's what you say. Everything that's happened tells me something else."

He tried again. "I was afraid to let wind of the oil get out. Vultures like Judge Andrews and McClintock would be all over you. Maybe I should have told you right away, but I only wanted to keep it quiet so McClintock couldn't try to cash in."

"That's no excuse! I had every right to know."

"It may be just a fluke. As a matter of fact, I've worked in oil fields, and I know there's never been any oil found around these hills. I was hoping to find a way to determine the amount and quality of the oil before I told you."

"Great, now you're a geologist. What else?"

Quinn felt her hurt, her anguish, as if they were his own. Maybe he *should* have told her about the oil. They could have tried to solve the problem together.

Maybe he *should* have told her how much he loved her and the twins. That he knew now they were more important to him than anything in his world. That she was the first woman he'd truly cared for, the first he was willing to change for. He couldn't bear to lose her now.

"It's none of your business, jailbird, so butt out." Richard McClintock strutted into view. "If there's any oil around here, it belongs to me."

Chapter Eleven

"I knew there was something going on here." Mc-Clintock shot Sara a smug smile. "Well, Miss High-and-Mighty, looks like you got yourself taken real good."

Rage swept over Quinn. Hands balled into fists, he started for McClintock. "How long have you been listening? I thought I told you to get the hell out of here!"

McClintock waved a legal-looking document at him. "Got myself a court order that says I can see my kids anytime I want. Now you can't stop me. I got the law on my side."

"Just try seeing the twins, and I'll spread what little brains you have over the landscape!"

McClintock stood his ground. "Oh yeah? You don't scare me. You're nothing around here. If Sara was dumb enough to let you get into her—"

His words changed abruptly into a startled squawk when Quinn grabbed him by the scruff of his neck and shook him until his teeth rattled.

"Hey, let go before I get the law on you!" McClintock gasped. "You got no call to attack me. You think you're so damn good, but you're nothing but a criminal. I know all about you, see," he taunted. "Lester told me everything. What do you think about that? Yeah, you think Sara will give you anything you want, now that..."

Quinn heard him through a red haze of fury. "You no-good, filthy bastard! I warned you what would happen if you didn't shut up and get out of here!" He drew back his arm and sent his fist crashing into McClintock's jaw.

"I don't care what you think you know about me, but don't you *ever* talk about Sara that way, you hear?" He shook his clenched fist at the fallen man. "She nursed your wife and took care of your children all these years while you were playing fast and loose with any money you could get your hands on. Sara deserves a lot better from you than the way you've been treating her."

McClintock struggled to get to his feet. Quinn put his foot on McClintock's shoulder and held him pinned to the ground. "You listening?" He waited until he got a reluctant nod. "No matter what you think, Sara's a lady, and you owe her." Quinn spit his words out between clenched teeth. "Not that you'd recognize a lady when you see one."

"Let go of him before you kill him!" Sara pushed Quinn away. "Not that I care, but the children are watching."

"Yeah. I'm their father and don't you forget it."
McClintock rubbed his jaw and scrambled to his feet.
"They wouldn't want to see anything happen to me."

Quinn snorted his disgust. "Biological father, that's
all."

"After what I just heard," McClintock sneered as
he mumbled through swollen lips, "sounds as if you're
the one who's trying to take Sara. Get rid of the guy,"
he commanded her, "I'm here now, and I'll take care
of things."

Quinn snarled his disgust. "Don't you ever give up?
Sara," he pleaded, "listen to me. Let me find out more
about the strike. You can decide what you want to do
about it later."

"You mean, *we'll* decide," McClintock announced.

Sara jabbed at his chest with both hands. "Understand this—the land belongs to me and the children.
I'll decide what to do with it."

"Not without me, you won't," McClintock pro-
tested. "I'm Amy's widower and the kid's father. I'll
decide what's good for them."

Sara fixed him with a cold stare. "In case you
weren't told by that no-account cousin of yours,
Amy's will named me the children's guardian. As for
the ranch, it belonged to me and Amy before you
married her. That lets you out of any ownership. Hell
will freeze over before I let you take the children or get
a piece of the ranch!"

"And as for you," she turned her cold gaze back to Quinn, "after you work off the rest of your sentence, you can leave."

"Tell him to get lost now, Sara," McClintock shouted. "You don't need him anymore."

"Why? Are you planning on finishing the fencing in his place?"

"Hell, no!"

"Then, he stays." She pointed to the lean-to. "Wait out there, Mr. Tucker."

Quinn was shocked at the reminder that he was still in her custody. The events of the past week, before he'd discovered oil, had erased any lingering bitterness he'd felt at being paroled to Sara. Her tender care of him since he'd been hit by too much sun had made him feel more like a welcome visitor than a hired hand. In his mind and in his heart, their romantic interludes had made them equals. How could she dismiss him like that after what they'd been to each other? How could she behave as if he were a stranger?

"Be sure and let me know when you change your mind." He threw his words at her as he hid the hurt that was tearing him apart. "You know where to find me."

McClintock danced a two-step in his excitement. "See, I told you the guy is nothing but trouble. Let me call the sheriff, Sara. He'll take care of him real good."

Quinn tore his gaze from Sara and started toward McClintock. "Haven't had enough?"

Sara pushed her way between Quinn and her brother-in-law. "That'll be enough from the both of you! Don't push your luck, Richard. You'd better get out of here while the getting is good."

"You haven't seen the last of me!" McClintock cursed and stalked away.

Sara started back to the house where Jase and Katie huddled together, their eyes riveted on their father.

Quinn's heart skipped a beat when he realized they had seen and heard too much. Just the thought of what they must be thinking sent a sinking feeling through him. They were so young, so vulnerable. No amount of explanations would set things right. He had to do something to bring order into their lives, even if it meant ignoring Sara's harsh words and coming back when his sentence was over.

The thought of losing Sara was unbearable. He'd try again to make his peace with her. But it would have to wait. He had to get rid of McClintock before he could settle the misunderstanding between them.

Quinn picked up the crumpled bills lying in the dirt, dusted them off and gazed sadly after Sara. The way she paused for a moment, head lowered, before she continued on to the house drove him to distraction. He'd wanted to make things easier for her, instead he'd made them worse. Knowing how much he'd added to her problems didn't help his state of mind.

He raised his eyes to the clear blue sky for guidance, shook his head and muttered his frustration.

After the tender moments they'd shared, he'd expected Sara to at least give him the benefit of the doubt. In his wildest dreams, he'd never envisioned a scene like this, or that he would lose the woman he'd come to care for so soon after finding her.

And the children. They'd become so close to being the family he'd never had. He'd never felt wanted or needed until now. Being around Sara and the twins had shown him what he'd missed; a home and family. He'd promised to take care of the twins, to come back to see them after his sentence was over, but now, after what they'd overheard, he'd be lucky if they wanted him around at all.

Coming back to visit no longer seemed enough. He wanted more; to be part of a family that included the three of them, Sara, Jase and Katie. The idea appealed to him as nothing ever had before.

He had to find Jase and Katie, explain what they'd heard and seen, tell them his side of the whole story before it was too late. He'd make them understand how sorry he was things had turned out this way, and then he'd find Sara and make her listen to him, too.

As he rounded the house, he saw McClintock and the twins by the apple tree. The louse hadn't left after all. Now that he'd heard about the oil, it was going to be hell getting rid of the leech.

McClintock held out a hand for Jase to shake. From the look of things, Jase wasn't having any part of him.

"C'mon, kid," McClintock scolded. "I've been away on business, but I'm back. I'm gonna take care of you from now on."

The twins backed away. "Aunt Sara takes care of us real good, Mr. McClintock," Jase said bravely.

"Now see here, kid! I'm your father, and that's what you'll call me!" He caught himself. "I'm more to you than your aunt. It's my job to see to it that no one takes you."

Katie began to cry. "I don't want anyone to take me. I want to stay here with Jase and Aunt Sara."

Her father threw up his hands and glared at her. "That's not what I meant. No one's going to take you anywhere. I just meant I'm not going to let anyone use you. I'm going to stay here with you. That's what I've been trying to tell you."

Katie cried harder. Jase pushed his way between her and his father. "We only need Aunt Sara to take care of us."

"Oh yeah? We'll see about that!"

Quinn had heard enough. At the sight of Katie's hunched and trembling shoulders and Jase's balled fists, a need to protect the twins drove caution to the winds. Trying to curb his anger, lest he frighten the children, he strode towards the trio. "That's enough, McClintock. Whatever you think you're entitled to, you'd better hash it out with your sister-in-law. And do it nicely, or you'll have me to answer to."

"We'll see about that," McClintock snapped at Quinn. "I'm going into town to tell my cousin that

Sara refused to honor the court order and that you attacked me. When I get back, those kids better straighten up!'' With the final threat, he stalked away.

Jase put his arm around Katie's shoulder and whispered words of comfort. "He's gone, Katie. Aunt Sara won't let him hurt us."

"And neither will I," Quinn added. "Come on over here and sit down. We have to talk." He led the way to the picnic table and waited with chagrin as the children kept their distance. When they eyed him warily and waited for him to speak, he felt like a heel. It looked as if they were afraid of him, too.

"I guess you guys are wondering what's going on around here and who's doing what to whom?"

Jase's troubled eyes fixed themselves on Quinn. "I was going to ask Aunt Sara."

"You do that, but first let me tell you where I fit in." He explained about finding the oil and why he'd hidden his discovery. He finally summed up the situation. "It's just that I thought your father might get back in the picture if he heard about the oil. I knew your aunt didn't want him around you."

He could see by their faces that the explanation didn't make the twins any happier. In their eyes, trouble was trouble, no matter who was causing it. "I'm working on getting rid of him. Things will be better, you'll see."

"We heard him tell Aunt Sara to make you leave right now, Mr. Tucker. Who's going to make him go away if you're not here?'' Twin sets of coffee-colored eyes bore into his.

"I'm not going, yet. We have plenty of time to worry about it later. I'm here, now."

He watched the play of emotions cross the children's faces. They were digesting his side of the story, but he could see they weren't convinced. "You can believe me. I'd never let anyone hurt you, I promise," he added. He desperately needed and wanted their trust.

Katie wiped away her tears with perfectly sculpted fingers. Jase held out his hand in his version of a manly handshake. "It's okay, Mr. Tucker. Don't worry about us. We have Aunt Sara. And she has us."

Quinn thoughtfully regarded the children. Jase's matter-of-fact statement worried him. He was afraid that, serious beyond their years, they were too ready to take matters into their own little hands.

SEVERAL HOURS LATER, Quinn was sitting on a bale of hay behind the barn and staring out at the horizon, mulling over his self-imposed newfound responsibilities.

"Miss Sara say come to dinner, Mr. Quinn."

"Dinner? You mean she's actually going to let me in the house? From the way she acted, I figured I'd be eating out here with Spike to keep me company."

"I do not understand everything, Mr. Quinn," Miguel said, his face a mask of sadness, "but Miss Sara is a good person, and you are not an animal like

Spike." A shy smile replaced the mask. "I think you
are a good person, too. No?"

"No, I mean yes." Quinn stretched and clapped
Miguel around the shoulders. The man's faith in him
renewed Quinn's resolve to get Sara to listen. "Thanks
for believing in me."

When Quinn came into the kitchen, it was unnatu-
rally quiet, the table set for one. Sara was setting a
salad on the table.

"Where are Jase and Katie?"

"I fed the twins and Miguel earlier."

"And you, Sara?" he asked quietly. "Have you
eaten, too, or don't you want to eat at the same table
with me?"

She shook her head. "I don't think I could eat now.
Maybe later."

Helplessly Quinn studied her. Her eyes were red, her
face was set in an expression that wrung his heart out
to dry. She looked cold, remote, as unlike the Sam he
had come to know as she could be.

"How far do you intend to go with this? Can't we
talk this over?"

"No. I'd rather keep this on a business basis."

Quinn stood his ground. "I'd like the chance to explain, to make you understand that I'm not the man I
was when we first met. I swear you can trust me. Just
give me a chance to help you."

"There's more to this than letting you help me get
rid of Richard. You hid something from me that you
knew I needed desperately. Why, I don't know. But

you've gotten all the chances you're going to get from me. You'll be gone soon and I'll be alone again. I might as well get used to the idea now."

"This isn't getting us anywhere." He rubbed the back of his neck. "Since trying to tell you I'm a changed man isn't enough, I guess I'll have to show you." He glanced at the bowl of stew she set before him. "I can eat later. Or, if I bother you that much, I'll take my plate outside."

Sara glared at him. "No, you won't. I expect you to act civilized as long as you're here. Sit."

Quinn swallowed his pride. He was glad to see Sara's eyes sparkle with anger. It was a far sight better than seeing her depressed.

It was no time to argue with her. He sat down.

He brightened as a thought struck him. If Sara was as angry or disappointed with him as she made out, he'd never be sitting at her kitchen table. There was more to this than she was letting on.

He purposefully lingered over his food. "Any more coffee?"

"Help yourself." He moved to the stove and poured himself a cup of unwanted coffee.

"The dinner was great. Best you've ever made."

"Thank you. It wasn't anything special." She avoided meeting his eyes while she cleared the table and stacked the dishes on the sink.

He expected an argument, but he forged ahead anyway. "It was to me. As a matter of fact, everything about you is special."

Her wary expression as she poured soap over the dirty dishes told him she hadn't forgiven him, but that she had something on her mind. He was in the mood to listen, and when she was through, he was going to make her return the favor.

Quinn took a dish towel from the rack over the sink. "Can I help you dry the dishes? I haven't been good for much else these past few days, but I'd like to be."

"Save the innuendoes, Mr. Tucker. They're wasted on me."

Sara could feel her self-control slipping with the subtle nuance in his voice, the double meaning in his words, intended or not. The butterflies in her stomach fluttered until she was afraid Quinn could hear the muted thunder.

Quinn *had* been good for her, and it had nothing to do with putting up fences. His very presence had made her feel safe, protected. His treatment of the children had been heartwarming to watch. As for the rest, his lovemaking had been unforgettable, had made her feel precious, loved, wanted.

She straightened her shoulders and willed the intoxicating images of her and Quinn making love to fade away. She had no place in her life for another man who broke her heart.

"This is the real world, not a dream." She gestured around her. "I took care of myself and the twins before you came here, and I'll do it again when you leave."

"Sam...Sara. I'm still here for you, if you let me."
He took her hands from the dishwater, let his fingers
slide over her soapy skin. The blush that covered her
gave her away, told him she was more aware of him
than she was willing to admit. He smiled sadly, lov-
ingly and dried her hands. "Sit down, Sara, let's talk."

"If only..." she began as she dropped into a chair.
"What's the use?"

She closed her eyes. In spite of her resolve to forget
Quinn, the kitchen faded away, replaced by images of
a bare chest bending over her, hard arms holding her,
a lithe body molding itself to hers, touching her in secret places. She wanted to throw her arms around his
neck, bury her face in his chest, feel his arms around
her, make her feel safe and warm. She couldn't. She
couldn't let him get that close to her again, not when
she was sure she was going to lose him.

"Sara, look at me." He gently touched her forehead until she opened her eyes. "If you really believe
I used you, you could have had me taken back to jail
in Juniper. Or even sent me on my way. But you
didn't. You let me stay, even fed me dinner. That must
mean something. You don't feed your enemy a good
meal. You feed him sandwiches like Sheriff Cable, or
you let him starve."

When she smiled sadly at his joke, some of the tension between them was broken. "I want to believe that
you feel something for me," he said. "It couldn't only
be that you needed me to help finish fencing the south
pasture that you're willing to keep me around."

She looked down at her clenched hands and slowly shook her head.

"Then what? If you're so angry with me, why do you want me to stay?"

"I'm not sure yet." She raised her troubled eyes to his. "But I'm not going to let myself be hurt again. Not by you, not by Richard, not by anyone. And I'm damned sure I'm not going to let the kids get hurt, either."

"I'd never hurt the kids, Sara. Or you."

"You already have."

"I talked to them. Explained why I kept quiet about finding the oil. They're bright, they seemed to understand. Why can't you?"

"I understand too much. Please don't get any more involved with the children," she pleaded. "It will only confuse them, hurt them more when you go. They'll have enough trouble coping with their father. Now that he knows there's oil here he won't walk away from it. Jase and Katie are afraid of him already. These arguments only make it worse."

"I'm sorry you feel this way." He rose and started to leave, a heaviness in his chest. He had come so close to finding the pot of gold at the end of the rainbow, a family to make his own. How could he lose it now?

"Quinn?"

Hope turned him back. "Yes?" The expression on her face made his gut constrict. He could see she was wound as tight as a drum. Whatever she had stopped him for, he could tell it took a lot of courage for her to speak.

"Did you mean what you said about caring for the twins?"

"Yes, and for you, too."

Sara wanted to believe him. Wanted to believe that he'd meant every word, every touch, every kiss they'd exchanged. But in the end, there was still the lie about the oil, and the children's welfare to consider.

The longing in his eyes, the way his hands were clenched by his sides, cried out for understanding. But her instincts warned her to be careful. She hardened her heart and looked away. Anywhere, but at him. She couldn't afford to take this kind of risk. It was more than a few nights of loving that was at stake. It was her future.

"I want you to forget what happened between us. It's over, and I don't intend for it to happen again. You're only going to be here a little more than a week, but I'd like to be able to trust you to watch over the twins while you're still here. Make sure their father doesn't bother them. Then, when your furlough is over, I want you gone."

"If that's the way you want it, you have my word. I'll watch over them." *And you, too.* Even as his heart begged him to try again to make her listen, to understand, pride made him leave.

Heartsick and worried more than he'd let on to Sara, Quinn strode out of the house. He'd never been in a situation where he felt responsible for other people before, but he was determined to be responsible for them now.

There was more at stake here than his future with Sara. Even if she didn't want anything more to do with him after next week, there was still Jase and Katie and his promise to get rid of their father. It was a promise he intended to keep.

He sat down on the steps and pondered his next move. He'd never been particularly lucky, unless you could call staying alive luck. He'd lived by his wits before, and he intended to live by them now.

Sara hurried by him, got into the truck and backed out of the yard without a word. Puzzled, he watched the faded blue vehicle disappear down the road. He breathed a sigh of relief. This was his chance to get in touch with Edwards, to find out if anyone knew McClintock and why he was hiding out at the Lazy M. Using the telephone in the house where Sara might find out was risky business, but he had no choice. Now that he'd sold his truck, he had no way to get into town.

Bill Edwards was waiting for his call.

"You're in luck, friend. That guy you asked about is on the payroll of a drug czar down in Mexico. He launders money by gambling with it in Vegas. Gets a percentage for doing it. The word is out on the street that he has some legal S.O.B. vouching for him every time the heat gets too close. The guy's got guts, what with the Feds and the gambling syndicates watching him."

"Hell, it's worse than I thought! McClintock must be hiding out here between deals."

"You got it. I don't envy the guy, he's going to be dead one of these days. The rumble is that he's been making a few mistakes lately. He's got both sides of the law just waiting to get him. Anything else you wanted to know about him?"

"That's more than enough, but keep it under your hat," Quinn said worriedly. "I don't want anyone coming around here and frightening Sara and the kids. Too bad their father doesn't feel the same way."

"Hey, I never heard of you."

"Nor I you." Quinn paused. "One more thing. I've got another favor to ask. If you find out anything more, or the name of the drug dealer McClintock works for, send it to a Tom Bregman in Juniper. He owns the town's drugstore. He'll see that I get it."

"Sure. Tell you what, I'll run it up to Bregman as soon as I can myself. Juniper is only an hour or so away from San Diego and I can use the fresh air. It sure sounds as if you could use a little help."

"More than you know, friend, more than you know. But keep a low profile. And say, I owe you a big one."

"Da nada, amigo."

Quinn hung up, went back outside and settled down to wait for what could possibly happen next.

He didn't have long to wait.

Chapter Twelve

"I've decided it's time to put you back to work, start-ing tomorrow." Sara planted her booted feet in front of Quinn's nose as he knelt in the kitchen garden.

He froze at the tone in her voice, dropped the car-rot seeds he was planting and rose to his full height. "I'm not your mule, Sara," he said quietly. "If you want me to go back to work on the fence, all you have to do is ask."

"Your parole papers are all I need. Asking isn't necessary. We'll start at sunup."

Maybe she had come on too strong, but she was firm in her resolve to distance herself from him. Foolish as it sounded, even to her, staying angry at him seemed to be the best way.

"Where are the children?" Ignoring Quinn, she checked the yard.

"The kids went into the house, said something about being hungry. You weren't back yet, so I fig-ured it was okay if they raided the cookie jar."

"I've already looked in the house." Worry lines appeared on her forehead. "It's not like the twins to disappear like that without telling someone where they're going."

Sara looked apprehensive as she searched the yard and saw only Miguel forking hay to a braying Spike. "Where could they can have gone off to?"

"I'm sure they're around somewhere. Prospecting for gold again, maybe." Quinn tried to keep things light, but the hair on the back of his head was starting to prickle. He had been so engrossed with planting, he hadn't noticed at least an hour had gone by since Jase and Katie had gone into the house.

"Where's Prince?"

"As a matter of fact, the pup followed the twins when they went in to clean up and get their cookies."

"No one's been around, have they?" she said over her shoulder as she started for the house.

"No, I've been watching the place. They must be somewhere around." Quinn sensed it was more than a cookie caper that had drawn them away. Especially if they took the pup along. "I'll come along and help you look again."

The children's bedroom was empty, too empty. Twin beds were neatly made up, clothing hung from pegs on a nautical shelf that had been nailed to one wall, small shoes were properly aligned. Things looked *too* tidy. The first thing Quinn noticed was that Katie's stuffed teddy bear and Jase's stuffed dog were nowhere to be seen.

"Sara," he said cautiously. "Where's the stuffed animals the kids drag around all the time?"

"They usually leave them on their pillows, when they go out-of-doors. The twins must have taken them with them wherever they've gone to." Her face turned white as she surveyed the spotlessly clean room. "Their room has never looked this tidy before. Something's wrong, I know it."

"Tell you what. I'll check the bathroom and the kitchen. You check the closets and the dresser drawers and see if anything else is missing."

Two minutes later, Quinn returned to find Sara still frantically searching the drawers and the closet.

"Anything else gone?"

"Some underclothes, sweaters, the animals."

"Well, it looks to me as if the twins have taken matters into their own hands and have run away."

"Run away!" Sara's complexion grew even more pale. "How do you know they've run away?"

"Easy," Quinn said sheepishly. "I've done it myself a time or two." *For most of my life.* "I had a feeling they were planning something. I even tried to talk them out of it, but it looks as if something pushed them over the edge. I could kick myself for not asking more questions and insisting on answers."

"You don't suppose they heard me telling you you had to leave, do you?"

"Who can tell with those two? All you have to do is listen to Jase and you know his mind is working faster than his tongue. Anyway, the cookie jar is empty, and the stack of shopping bags you had in the pantry are all over the pantry floor." He laughed in spite of his fears. "Right smart packing, I'd say. Clean drawers and cookies for comfort. Not bad, for a couple of four-year-olds."

"How can you joke at a time like this?" The tears that had welled in her eyes spilled over onto her cheeks.

"It's better than crying." He longed to wipe the tears from the corner of her eyes, but he was still teed off with the way she'd ordered him back to work. But, first things first. He'd find the twins and then make it clear to Sara that she *had* to listen to him. Make her understand that he'd had her best interests at heart all along. "Get the truck, and some blankets. Maybe even something hot to drink. I'll tell Miguel we're going to be gone for a while."

"Where are we going?"

"Out to find the kids. We'll try the road south first. Jase's listened to so many of Miguel's stories, I have a hunch that the kid will try for the Mexican border."

Sara stifled a cry. "You're not making this any better, you know. You talk as though the children are criminals trying to get out of the country."

"Don't worry. Four-year-old feet can't get very far."

"What do you mean, don't worry? There are animals out there!"

"Relax, they don't stand a chance against Jase. He's not afraid of anything, remember? Besides, it looks as if they took the pup along for company."

He didn't want to frighten Sara, but he prayed silently to the guardian who watched over children. It was getting dark and there were predators out there, some of them human. He had to find them tonight, and soon.

IT WAS THE LONGEST NIGHT she'd ever spent. Between trying to keep an eye out for two small escapees and attempting to stay calm, she'd soon realized things weren't going to be as easy as Quinn was trying to make her believe.

"Maybe you were wrong about the children running away. You don't suppose Richard has them, do you?" She felt an overwhelming guilt for taking the truck and vanishing long enough for something to have happened to Jase and Katie. But she'd had to get away by herself so she could do some serious thinking. She'd put her own needs before that of the twins. Now, they might be paying the price for her selfishness.

"One thing for certain, Jase is apparently smart enough not to stay on the main road, or else they've gotten tired and are holed up somewhere." Quinn stopped the truck and jumped out to investigate a suspicious pile by the side of the road. "Trash," he said in disgust as he returned to the truck. "Someone's dumped a couple of garbage bags. There ought to be a law."

Sara thought of the distance the twins could have walked from the time they'd left the ranch. No more than a few miles, at best, but maybe too many for such young feet. Dear Lord, she prayed, the children are so small, so vulnerable. Please let them be safe.

"Any ranches around here? The kids could have taken shelter with friends."

"A few, but no one the children could have known that well."

"That might not stop Jase, except that..." His voice trailed off.

"Except?" Sara grabbed his arm. "Except what?"

"Maybe they don't want to be found. No, my hunch is that they're still out here, somewhere. We'll find them," he assured her as he heard her sob of fear. "Don't worry, Sara. We'll find them."

"We have to. I'll never forgive myself if they've gotten hurt or if Richard has them."

"I'm sure you would have known by now if McClintock took them. It doesn't do any good to worry about them getting hurt, either. We'll find them."

They drove slowly down the road for several miles, backtracking over narrow county roads and stopping frequently to call to the children. Several hours passed.

Quinn finally stopped. "Driving in circles isn't getting us anywhere. They're not on the roads, or we would have found them by now. What else is around here where they could go to hole up?"

She stared into his eyes, finally remembering the place the children loved so well; the one place she and Quinn had made their own. The place she'd driven to this afternoon to do her thinking. She finally whispered, "The oasis? They love to go there to watch the squirrels."

"It's in the other direction." Quinn seemed to consider the possibility. "But you may be right. It's worth a try."

He turned the truck around and drove toward Juniper until he found the cutoff to the oasis. He drove slowly, searching for some evidence the twins had been here.

The truck's headlights shone on the shallow water pond. As soon as Sara's eyes grew accustomed to the glare of the headlights, she made out Jase and Katie huddled together in a nest of sweaters and stuffed animals, sleeping. Prince, standing guard at their feet, raised his head and growled a low warning.

"We must have passed each other on the road," she said brokenly. "I was here this afternoon." She struggled to open the cab door.

"Strange place to visit, isn't it?" Quinn said as he reached over her and opened the door.

Sara looked at him mutely. She couldn't tell him she'd come here to say goodbye.

She scrambled out of the cab and headed toward the sleeping children. "Jase, Katie, sweethearts, wake up," she cried as she knelt and gathered them into her arms. "Are you all right?"

"Aunt Sara?" Jase rubbed sleepy eyes. He looked up and saw Quinn standing silently behind his aunt. "Hello, Mr. Tucker."

"Are you all right, Jase? Katie, too?" Sara repeated, as she kissed him, lifted him and smothered him in her relief. She was stopped by Quinn's hand on her shoulder.

"We have to come to an understanding, first. Otherwise this might happen again." After a pregnant pause, he leaned down for a man-to-man confrontation.

"I thought we agreed that you were going to trust me to put things right for all of us?"

"Yes, sir. But—"

"No 'buts.' Running away from problems never solved a thing. Believe me, I know. Think you can remember that?"

"Yes, sir," Jase answered bravely. "Can I say something, Mr. Tucker?"

"What is it, Jase?"

"I'm glad you and Aunt Sara found us." He put a hand in Quinn's. "I didn't want to scare Katie, but I was kinda lost, or I would have come back."

"I'm glad we found you, too."

Just the thought of the two little ones wandering around in the dark struck terror in Sara's heart. She was filled with a fierce desire to comfort Jase instead of lecturing him.

"I don't think now is the time for this talk with Jase." Sara gathered a sleepy Katie and held her so her head rested on her shoulder. "It's enough that we found them."

"That's where you're wrong. He'll realize what he's done if we discuss the problem while it's still fresh in his mind." Quinn gently ruffled Jase's hair, then hugged him again. "Now he'll understand how much he's frightened you by taking matters into his own hands."

Jase squared his shoulders. "I'm sorry, Aunt Sara."

"Why did you run away, Jase?" Sara asked. "Why didn't you come and tell me what was bothering you?"

Jase shuffled his feet, shrugged his shoulders. "We heard our father say he had the right to visit us anytime he wanted, and then we heard you tell Mr. Tucker he had to leave. You were so mad, we knew you meant it. We were afraid that our father would come back to take us and there wouldn't be anyone to stop him."

"And you think I'm the only one able to do that?"

"Yes sir, Mr. Tucker. You made him go away before."

"Don't worry, Jase. I won't let you down. Now, into the truck and cover up with this blanket. Let's get on back home and get a good night's sleep." Quinn picked up Prince and set him in the cab, too. "This pup is the last dog I ever thought would make a good watchdog. We'll have to buy him something special for taking such good care of you. Good dog." Prince licked Quinn's hand and gazed up at him with soulful eyes.

Cradling Katie in her arms, Sara watched the byplay between Quinn and the puppy. There was something about Quinn that drew not only children to him, but animals, too. She was grateful to him, but he still had to leave. She couldn't afford to have him around. He'd only break the children's heart when he ultimately left. *And, maybe, hers.*

Safely home, and with Quinn's help, Sara put the children into bed, clothes and all. Even Prince came in for some TLC. Tucking the blanket closer around a sleepy Jase, she kissed him and Katie good-night and stood back for Quinn to do the same.

"Aunt Sara, will you turn the night-light on?"

"You bet." Tears were flowing from her eyes by the time she left the room and joined Quinn in the hall. Behind her, she could hear Prince jump into bed with Jase, but she didn't have the heart to order the dog back to the floor. She owed him so much.

"I don't know how to thank you for helping me find the children. It was all my fault. I shouldn't have gone off and left them."

Quinn wanted to reach out and pull her to him, but he knew she would brush him away. "Don't let what happened get to you. You've been a good mother to the twins."

"I don't know. I love them so much, and all I did was cause them pain by fighting with you and telling you to leave out in the open where they could hear me."

"You did what you thought was right at the time. That's all anyone can do. They love you very much, Sara Ann Martin. Don't sell yourself short."

"I should have watched my temper, then this wouldn't have happened."

"I'm sure they aren't going to hold it against you. They're only children."

"Thank you for your help."

"No problem. I care for the little ones, too. He couldn't stop himself from stroking her golden hair. "As for us, we still have unfinished business to take care of."

She shook her head. "Not as far as I'm concerned." she said, effectively thrusting away the warm empathy that had begun to flow between them.

HE WAS LETTING a fence pole slide into place, and congratulating himself at his expertise, when the sound of a car horn turned him around. A station wagon came careening across the dry grass and jolted to a stop. Tom Bregman jumped out. Shading his eyes, he came toward them, waving. Quinn waved back and hurried over to Bregman's side.

"What's your hurry, Tom." He laughed. "Someone chasing you?"

"Howdy, Quinn. You're right there. Sara's brother-in-law and Lester Andrews are right behind me." He handed over an envelope to Quinn and fanned himself with his hat. "Fellow showed up just as I was getting ready to open the store. He was so set on my giving this to you right away, I figured I'd better get out to the ranch as fast as I could. Miguel told me where you were."

"Thank you, Tom." Quinn shook the man's hand. "I'm grateful to you for going to the extra trouble."

"No trouble at all. Saw McClintock and Andrews getting into their car as I drove by. Never drove so fast in my whole life."

Only half hearing, Quinn tore open the envelope and scanned its contents. Bill Edwards had come through.

Sara came up behind him. "Hi, Tom. What brings you here?"

"Sara, read this."

The puzzled expression on Sara's face grew as she read a copy of a geologist's report. "Where does this come from?"

"I asked a guy I worked with up at the Bakersfield oil fields to see if he could find anything on an oil survey on this part of the state. He found that and sent me a copy through Tom. Do you see what it says?"

"It says we're standing on an oil field too small and with too poor a grade of oil to be profitable. If that's true, I don't see what having oil on the property is going to do for me. I'm still dirt poor."

"Sara," Quinn added softly. "It means we can put the oil behind us and work together to find another solution to your financial problems."

"I've already found it." She gestured to the unfinished fence line. "Anyway, I can't feel badly over losing something I never had." She glanced at the geological report. "But at least, it looks as if you were telling me the truth. So it's back to the fences."

Tom Bregman cleared his throat. "I think that'll have to wait a bit, folks." He gazed over Quinn's shoulder. "Company's coming."

A late-model luxury car came bumping across the grass and slid to a stop alongside the wagon. Richard McClintock and his cousin the judge poured out the doors. Andrews led the way.

"I hear you've violated the terms of your work-furlough parole, Tucker," he said as he came to a stop in front of Quinn.

"Oh?" Quinn dug his heels into the ground and folded his arms across his chest. "Since I never saw any paperwork, what terms would those be?"

"You were here on probation. If you caused any trouble, the furlough was over. But you outsmarted yourself when you used the situation to get friendly with Sara, here. Friendly enough to try to bilk her out of her fortune," Andrews lectured in his best judicial manner. "From the way I hear it, things look pretty serious to me. And since you already have a record, it's serious enough to run you out of town. We know how to take care of con men around here."

Quinn eyed him with disgust. "My record says I paid the price for being too young and too dumb to stay out of trouble. As for my trying to con Sara out of the fortune she doesn't have, you're going to have to prove it."

"No problem." Andrews gestured at McClintock. "I've got a witness who heard you try to sweet-talk her out of her land."

"You've got a hotheaded moron who doesn't know what he's talking about," Quinn retorted. He fixed McClintock with an angry stare. "If you're looking for more trouble, McClintock, I'm just the man to help you find it," he called over the judge's shoulder.

Andrews started forward. "Now see here, Tucker, you're not making your case any better by that kind of talk."

Sara muttered her disgust and stepped in front of the judge. "Lester, I think we'd better have a talk before you make a fool of yourself."

"Sara's right, Lester," Bregman interjected. "Better listen to her. From what I know, you owe her and Tucker an apology."

"An apology! When he's trying to steal my kids' inheritance and make me look like an ass?" McClintock shot angry looks at Quinn from behind his cousin's back. "If Sara wants to let Tucker make a fool of her, that's her business. The kids are my business. I'm not going to let anyone rob them!"

Sara marched up to Andrews, pushed him aside and jabbed her brother-in-law in the ribs with both hands. "Listen to me and listen carefully, Richard McClintock. The children are *my* business. You gave up your rights to them when you left four years ago. You weren't listening when I told you *I* have legal custody of them, now." Her voice shook with anger. "As for letting anyone take advantage of me, your rotten mind has been working overtime!"

"Now see here, Sara," Andrews broke in. "My cousin's only trying to do what's best for his children. As the law in Juniper, it's my duty to investigate what's going on here."

Sara tore her gaze from her brother-in-law and threw Andrews a disgusted grimace. "Nothing's going on. Quinn and I are trying to finish fencing the south pasture of the ranch so I can board horses. You're holding us up."

"What about the oil, Sara?" McClintock broke in. "What about the oil? You're not going to keep that all for yourself, you know."

Goaded into action, Quinn grabbed the geologist's report out of Sara's hand and thrust it under Judge Andrews's nose. "Read it for yourself, Your Honor. If you still want to lock me up or run me out of town on a trumped-up charge, do it after I finish the fencing. Until then..." His voice trailed off as he gestured to the automobiles. "Sara and I have to get back to work."

A deep silence fell as Andrews studied the report. He cleared his throat. "Well, it does looks like there isn't much oil, after all. But," he added ominously, "that doesn't change anything. You're still guilty of assaulting my cousin when all he was trying to do was to visit with his children. And with my written permission. We don't need your kind around here." Pausing, he pronounced, "I hereby convene court and

I'm commuting your sentence, Quinn Tucker. Pack your things and get out of town, now."

At a simultaneous outburst of protest from Quinn and Sara, Bregman took Andrews by the shoulder. "Why don't we get out of here, Lester, and leave the folks to finish the job of fencing the pasture. Unless you really want the man to leave?" Through raised eyebrows, he waited for Andrews to make up his mind.

The judge frowned and shook off Bregman's hand. "Of course I do. I just said so, didn't I?"

"Still stubborn as a mule, aren't you, Lester? Well, since I heard Tucker sold his truck to Bob Foster, I'll just hang around and run him into town to the bus stop."

"I'll give you permission to do that, but he'd better be on the next bus out of town."

Bregman shrugged. "Yes, Your Honor." He waited until McClintock and Andrews got into their car and drove away.

"Guess you want to say goodbye to Sara. Meet you at the car, son."

Quinn studied Sara. "Well, it looks as if you're getting your wish, even if it is a little sooner than expected. Too bad it couldn't wait until the fences were finished." He put his tools in the truck bed. "It's been an interesting few weeks, anyway."

"Interesting!" Sara planted her hands on her hips and glared at him. "Is that all you have to say?"

He wiped his hands on a rag and faced her. "What do you want me to do? Thank you for some of the best days and nights in my life? Or kiss you goodbye and beg you to let me stay? Not after the way you've been acting. I don't have to beg any woman to—''

"That's enough! Your rotten temper is showing again!"

"Sara, it's either be mad as hell or kiss you sense-less. I'm already angry enough to do both, but I don't think it's time for a kissing contest."

"Why, you big jerk! No wonder you're a drifter. No decent person would have you around! And further-more, at the rate you lose your temper, you're head-ing for trouble again."

"Trouble's been my middle name for as long as I can remember," he rejoined. "I'm used to it. By the way, Ms. Martin, you've got a pretty good temper of your own, too."

"I don't want to hear any more. Just go. Tom can stop at the house long enough for you to pick up your things, but I don't want to see you there when I get back!"

Quinn glared at her, spun on his heel and stalked over to where the druggist was waiting for him. "That damn woman, I don't know what I see in her!" he muttered as he got into the car.

"Seems to me that the two of you care for each other, or you wouldn't be able to get each other riled up so much," Bregman laughed. "Two of a kind, that's what you are."

Sara watched the car disappear from sight, taking with it the man she cared for, the last man on earth she should care for. A feeling of emptiness set in, growing larger as the image of the car grew smaller.

She glanced around the pasture, at the unfinished fences, and at Miguel's old hat that Quinn left lying at her feet. She picked it up, held it to her breast. Tears fell as she mourned for her loss and for the loss of the twins' dream.

"I'LL DROP YOU OFF at the house and then take you to the bus stop. You *are* going to come back, aren't you?"

"Soon, I hope. I couldn't let on to Sara, but I'm coming back to clear up a few things."

"Looked to me back there like she was pretty angry. Might run you off the place if you showed up again."

"One thing I've learned, Tom, is that the best defense is a good offense. Sara's on the ropes. She doesn't know what she wants, but I intend to show her."

"I'll look forward to it. Sara needs a strong man in her life. By the way, Edwards left me another envelope. Said it was for your eyes only."

Quinn opened the envelope, scanned its contents and broke into a wide smile.

Chapter Thirteen

As soon as the bus disappeared down the highway to San Diego, Quinn went into the tiny crossroads gas station. The lanky man bending over an ancient truck straightened up.

"Howdy. What can I do for you?"

"Got a car to rent?"

"Name's Davis. Take a look around, young feller. See any automobiles?"

Quinn gazed around the old wooden structure. Fifty years' worth of gasoline- and oil-covered, discarded auto parts and used tires. The only vehicle in sight was the old truck Davis had been working on.

"Name's Tucker. No, don't think I do, unless you think that truck qualifies. Does it run?"

"Course it runs, just like a clock. Owned it for twenty-five years."

"Sounds good. Is it for rent?"

Davis glanced at the truck, then back to Quinn. "Depends on where you want to drive it. Wouldn't like to have it gone for long."

"Just up the road to Juniper. I'll have it back to you in two days. Guarantee it."

"Thirty dollars a day, not a penny less."

"Mr. Davis, it's worth every penny. I'll take it." Quinn counted out the money. "Fill 'er up."

"Cost you another twenty. Gas ain't cheap, you know."

"I know." Quinn tried to look suitably impressed as he handed over another bill.

He slowly drove to Juniper at the maximum thirty miles an hour the truck could handle without starting to cough. He was in no hurry to get to town before dark, anyway. His business with Andrews was better conducted where eyes couldn't see and ears couldn't hear.

He remembered Cable going to get the judge after he'd handcuffed him and left him to wait in the police car. It didn't take him long to find Judge Andrews's house. It was with a great deal of satisfaction that he mounted the steps to the judge's old turn-of-the-century mansion. A discreet bronze plaque announced that the judge performed marriages on the weekends. Drawn curtains and a locked screen door greeted Quinn. Obviously guests weren't welcome today. He pounded on the door.

Persistence paid off. Andrews was home and crankier than ever.

"Oh, it's you, is it? I thought I ran you out of town this morning. What are you doing around here?"

Quinn was interested to note Andrews's voice had lost some of its judicial resonance. It sounded as if the judge were none too pleased with the way things were shaping up. Too bad.

He could understand why Andrews was a scowling mess. Anyone who had to put up with a cousin like McClintock had a problem on his hands. "I was looking for your cousin, and you, too, for that matter. Can I come in?"

Andrews glanced behind Quinn to make certain he was alone before he unlatched the screen door. Reluctantly he stepped aside so Quinn could enter.

"Your cousin here, Judge?"

"Upstairs. Not that it's any of your business," he answered. "Why?"

"Anyone else home?"

"No. Say your piece and get the hell out of here before I arrest you again. And this time, there isn't going to be a cushy work-furlough program waiting for you. You'll rot in jail where you belong."

"Don't worry, I don't plan on staying long. I've something to say to you and your cousin, and I didn't think you'd care to have anyone else hear about it."

"And just what fool nonsense are you talking about?"

"In a minute. Mind getting McClintock down here?"

After shouting for his cousin to get himself downstairs, Lester Andrews led the way into his study. "It was a sorry day when you decided to break the law in

Juniper, Tucker. You've been a pain in the ass ever since I first laid eyes on you.''

Quinn snorted. ''I never intended to visit Juniper. It was all your fool sheriff's idea.''

''Now, just what is it you think I might be interested in?'' The angry judge gestured to McClintock to come into the room.

Quinn made himself at home. Andrews's ruddy complexion paled when Quinn spoke a single name. ''DeVallera.''

Andrews glared at him. ''Just what the hell is that name supposed to mean to me?''

''Yeah, what's that supposed to mean?'' McClintock stood glaring in the doorway.

''Shut up, Richard. Let me handle this.''

McClintock sauntered into the room. ''He's bluffing, Lester. He doesn't know anything.''

''Really? Then how do you know I'm bluffing?''

''Richard, I told you to shut up and I mean it!''

''What would you say if I told you that your no-account cousin here—'' Quinn gestured at a glowering McClintock ''—makes a living laundering cash for a drug syndicate headed by Enrique DeVallera down below the border. And does it by gambling in Vegas?''

''Ridiculous!''

''Not only that, he keeps more than his cut.''

''I'd call you a liar.''

''And that every time the law gets too close, Your Honor, you vouch for him?''

"I still say you're a liar. Now, get the hell out of here or I'll arrest you for trespassing."

"I don't think so. Especially since you get a hefty cut for fronting for McClintock here."

"You're dreaming."

"It does sound like a nightmare, all right." Quinn leaned forward and spoke in measured tones. "And furthermore, I know that McClintock needs the ranch to hide out for a while. The children are only an excuse. He doesn't give a damn about them, but it does make for a good reason to be here, doesn't it?"

"You asking, or telling? Either way, you're stabbing in the dark. Get out."

"No, sir. I've got all the proof I need, anytime I want it. You'd better make certain I don't want it. If I have to go that far, you're both finished and so is the judicial job you have."

"The hell you say!"

Quinn rose. "I'm warning you both to leave Sara and the twins alone. And, as long as you have that attitude, *judge,* I'd suggest you tender your resignation as soon as possible before you get thrown out of office for moral turpitude. In fact, maybe the two of you want to take a vacation where neither DeVallera or the Feds can find you. Do the rest of Juniper a favor and take Cable with you."

McClintock stuttered his indignation. "You can't make me give up the ranch!"

"The ranch, eh? What happened to this sudden desire you had to be a father?"

"Better watch out," McClintock blustered, "you ain't going to get anywhere threatening me! I've got connections."

"Try me," Quinn said in disgust. "Just try me. Oh, and by the way, I'm not alone in this. I've got connections, too. If anything happens to me or Sara and the kids, you're gone. Both of you."

Satisfied that he'd put the fear of God into the two, Quinn left the house. He stood on the steps and took a deep breath. The mountain air in Juniper was going to get a lot cleaner, soon.

As he ran down the steps to the ancient truck, Quinn drew a relieved breath. He'd promised Sara there wouldn't be any violence, and he'd kept his promise. Now, he could go back to her with clean hands.

"WHERE'S MR. TUCKER, Aunt Sara?"

Sara hesitated. How could she tell him Quinn was gone and they'd probably not see him again? She dried the last of the dinner dishes and sank into a chair. Worried expressions on their faces, Jase and Katie waited by the door for her answer. Even Prince managed to look anxious as he dropped to the floor, put his nose between his paws and stared reproachfully at her.

She knew that the twins would be heartbroken if she told them the truth; Quinn had been run out of town by Judge Andrews.

Afraid that they might take it into their heads to go find him, she fabricated a story.

"Quinn's work-furlough was over. He had to leave, but he told me to tell you he's sorry he couldn't stay."

"Why didn't he say goodbye?"

"He wanted to, but he couldn't." Blinking back her tears, Sara reached out to hug the children to her. How could she comfort Jase and Katie when her own heart was near to breaking?

"Does that mean our father is coming back, Aunt Sara?" The usually silent Katie looked up at her aunt. "I don't want him to."

"No!" She could feel the fear in the children's voices, see it in their eyes. "And if he tries, I'll..." Her voice trailed off. What *would* she do if he did come back? Especially when Andrews was clearly on his side? "We'll just take one day at a time, shall we?"

Jase and Katie looked at each other. Even the dog sensed something was wrong. As if to remind them he was there, Prince rubbed his nose against their legs.

"Do you remember what Mr. Tucker told you? To talk things over with me before you do anything?" When the children remained silent, she added, "He wouldn't like it if you take matters into your own hands again."

"We won't, Aunt Sara. But we don't understand why he had to leave."

"Trust me, Jase. Everything is going to be all right. Just trust me." They nodded, but she could see the reluctance in their faces.

"Tell you what, why don't we get out the tub and you can take a bath right here in the kitchen?" When they agreed, she told them to go and get their bath toys. It wouldn't make up for Quinn's loss, but she had to distract them somehow. And herself, too, before she gave herself away.

It was the second time she'd lost a man she'd loved, although nothing she'd felt for Steven Miles had come close to what she felt for Quinn. Steven had left her. She'd planned to send Quinn away before he had a chance to leave her, too. Before he decided to move on and break her heart.

What was there about her that made her so easy to leave?

She filled the tub with tepid water, dropped in lemon-scented bubble bath. "Come on, you two," she called. "No, not you, Prince. You can watch for now. Your turn will come later."

Holding Prince, she knelt on the floor beside the tub. The children giggled at the way he kept trying to squirm out of her hands and into the water.

"No, you don't." Sara laughed. "You can have a bath later. Dogs do *not* bathe in the same water as humans!"

Jase and Katie exchanged glances and, before Sara knew what was going to happen, splashed handfuls of soapy water over her and Prince. "Now they do, Aunt Sara!"

"I'll get you guys for that!" Sara reached out, grabbed a flying foot and tickled Katie until she squealed. Jase got even by splashing more water over her and the linoleum floor. Prince barked and ran in circles around the tub.

When no one answered his knock, Quinn let himself into the kitchen. The sight of Sara and the twins roughhousing on the wet floor brought a broad smile to his face and a warm glow in his chest. This was what a family should be like, he thought. This was the kind of family a man should have.

"Mr. Tucker!" Jase almost leapt from the tub. "You came back!"

Sara grabbed him around the knees before he managed to climb over the edge of the tub. "Careful, there's soapy water everywhere. You could fall and hurt yourself!"

Quinn eyed the water on the floor, the excited twins, and a very wet Sara. "Tell you what, why don't you go on up and change into something dry, Sara? I'll take over. A bath's a bath, after all. Shouldn't be too difficult to finish the job."

Sara sank back on her knees. "Where did you come from?"

"I never really left. I just took care of some unfinished business."

"Richard?" she mouthed, pointing to the gaping twins.

He nodded. "You have my word, everything's going to be okay from now on."

"Wow, Mr. Tucker. Does that mean you're going to stay?"

"We'll see, Jase. Now, do I get to supervise this party, or not?"

"You do. I'll go change." Sara touched his hand in passing. "And thank you, for the other."

Small moving bodies, rubber ducks, tiny boats and empty plastic bottles crowded the tub. Quinn took a swipe at a flurry of arms and legs, upturned noses and grinning mouths as they swam past him, splashing him with lemon-scented water. When he was thoroughly soaked, he gave up.

"Okay, guys, that's enough for tonight. We'll organize this operation better tomorrow." He grabbed one slippery body at a time, wrapped it in towels, and sat back to dry himself off. "Go get your pajamas and hop in bed."

"We're not tired, Mr. Tucker."

"Maybe not, but I am," Quinn said firmly. "Off with you, while I dry myself."

He could hear giggles floating down the stairs. He thought about what lay ahead of him. Days of children's laughter, evenings of baths and bedtime stories, and nights of loving Sara, or drifting on? Choices, but no choice, when it came right down to it. A life with Sara and the children was something he wanted more than empty days and lonely nights.

Drying his hair on an extra towel, he hummed a tune he remembered from somewhere in the past, something about it being so nice to come home to the one you loved. After years of drifting, he had come home to the one he loved, and Sara was that woman.

Sara came back into the kitchen. Fresh jeans and a T-shirt hugged her figure. Her hair hung loosely over her shoulders. "I wasn't expecting you to come back."

"I came back for them," he said gesturing upstairs. "And for you." When moisture sprang into her eyes, he felt like a heel. "Hey, Sam. I didn't mean to make you cry. The last thing I want to do is to cause you any more heartache." He wiped her tears away with a corner of the towel. "This is going to be the last time you're going to cry, if I have anything to do about it."

Sara smiled through her tears. "The children missed you."

"Only the children?"

Her heart in her eyes, Sara asked, "Are you going to stay a while?"

"As long as you'll have me. But first, I have to tell you about your brother-in-law." He told her how he found out about McClintock laundering drug money, and Andrews's participation, and what he'd done about it. "They're not going to be around much longer to bother you or anyone else. I'll see to that." He hesitated. "If you still want me around."

"You'd better go on up and change into something dry if you intend to stay," Sara replied, face hidden in the towel.

"If that's a yes, I will, but first I have something else to tell you. About the oil…" He hesitated, took a deep breath and made his confession. "That geological survey report was a phony."

Sara looked up in surprise. "A phony? How?"

"I had one faked to get rid of your brother-in-law. But, before you get too angry, I know enough about oil to be sure it'll turn out to be true. We can find out when things quiet down. Just trust me, Sara?"

She gazed into his eyes for a long moment. He could see the struggle to believe him, to depend on his word. When her face cleared and she nodded, he leaned forward and kissed her gently. "Thank you. We've found something better than oil, haven't we, Sara? We found each other."

Before she had a chance to answer, Jase called, "Aunt Sara! We're ready for our bedtime story."

Sara laughed shakily. "Sorry. I have to go."

"I'd like to read to them tonight, if it's all right with you."

"You want to read storybooks?" Amused, Sara shook her head. "You don't know what you're getting into."

"I'm going to find out. After all, I need to get in practice."

"There's a stack of books on their nightstand. Right now, *Three Billy Goats Gruff* is their favorite."

"Okay, you guys," Quinn announced as he came through the bedroom door. "If you play your cards right, I'm going to read to you tonight instead of your aunt."

Jase stared at him. "Mr. Tucker, does that mean you're going to be our dad?"

"Dad?" Quinn was taken by surprise. That was the question of the hour, but how did this young-old sprite know? "What makes you ask?"

"Because that's what dads are supposed to do, aren't they, Katie?"

Katie nodded and put her hand in Quinn's. The expectant look on her face brought a resolve to his heart. If ever a little girl deserved to have a loving father, it was Katie. And if ever a man needed children like her and Jase in his life, it was him.

"I don't know, Jase," Quinn answered. "I never was lucky enough to have mine read to me. But, I'm game to read to you if you want me to." His heart swelled with pleasure when the twins nodded. He took a deep breath and got started.

"...Then big Billy Goat Gruff went across the bridge to eat grass. The three goats ate and ate. If the grass is still there, the goats are still eating."

"That's some story." Quinn tried to look suitably impressed. "Shows you can get rid of the bad guys if you're determined enough, even if you're a goat. You see, the troll tried to keep the goats from getting across the bridge to eat grass, and they kept trying until they did. The idea of the story is that if you want something badly enough, you can do anything."

Jase and Katie looked solemn. "Like you when you made us safe, Mr. Tucker?"

"Like me, Jase. You made me feel safe, too," Quinn answered as he soothed a damp lock of hair away from Jase's forehead. "In fact, you know, I don't think I've ever felt so safe before."

"Do you want us enough?" Katie asked.

"More than that." Quinn kissed her pert nose. "I needed a little boy and little girl for my own, but I didn't realize how much until I met the two of you."

"We'll be yours if you want us to be." Katie snuggled into his arms. "And Aunt Sara will, too. I'll ask her, if you want."

"That's a nice thought, Katie, but some things a man has to do for himself. Thanks for the offer, ladybug. Now, it's off to sleep for you so I can get to it."

He found her in the kitchen, straightening things that didn't need straightening, folding and unfolding damp towels. He would have to take it gently, to start all over again.

"Sara?"

She started, looked up and stared at him across the room. "Are the children in bed?"

"Yes. Sara, I…" The wary look in her eyes stopped him. What was she afraid of? For that matter, what was he afraid of? It was time to put her fears to rest, to tell her how much he loved her, wanted to stay. If she'd have him. But words would not be enough.

He swept her into his arms and carried her upstairs to the room they'd shared once before. Under the probing demand of his kisses, her defenses crumbled.

"Quinn," she murmured as tendrils of sensation tangled her thoughts and wrapped her in sweet, sensual bonds of pleasure. "I was so afraid you were never going to come back to me."

He lifted his eyes to hers. "I never intended to stay away. I just couldn't tell you until I straightened out a few things that should make it safe for you and the kids." He bent to kiss the hollow between her breasts. "I want to spend the rest of my life showing you how much you mean to me."

He slowly drew her T-shirt from her willing body, then her jeans. He kissed her through her lacy bra, and again when he'd unhooked it and thrown it aside.

She was on fire. "You, too," she whispered in the darkness as she unbuttoned his shirt and waited for him to take off the rest of his clothing. "I want to feel you, touch you, taste you." She ran her hands over his lithe body and fingered the dark curls on his chest that fascinated her so. He was the man she'd been waiting for all her life.

He imprisoned her arms while his lips turned her skin to flames. Crouching at her feet, he kissed her instep, her toes, the inside of her thighs. His mouth nuzzled her flesh, his tongue was strong and demanding. Gasping, she stopped him with a kiss. "Quinn, please," she murmured against his lips.

"Soon," he answered.

His fingers explored her, stroking her. Her sensitive skin was alive to him as he stroked her until she cried out. When they moved together, skin to skin, heartbeat to heartbeat, it was the fulfillment of all her dreams.

As THE SUNLIGHT CREPT in the window, Sara stretched luxuriously. Memories of the night brought her wide awake. Sitting up, she cautiously leaned over the still-sleeping Quinn, surprised at his vulnerability in sleep. There were a hundred sides to this man. If they spent their whole life together, he'd always surprise her. And excite her. A smile twitched at the corner of her mouth. Maybe that was the secret of his attraction for her. Within this steady, loyal stubborn man was a wellspring of humor that would last through the hard times.

A smile touched his face. His lips moved. She leaned closer to hear what he was saying in his sleep. "Sam."

"What about Sam?" she whispered.

"I found her last night."

With a start, Sara realized Quinn was teasing her again. Before she knew what was happening, strong arms shot out, captured her and pulled her down over his chest.

"Hello, Sam," he said with an endearing smile.

Sara could feel her heart pounding. Desire flowed through her veins like liquid fire. His fingers lightly caressed her cheek before he kissed her with lips tender, yet demanding.

He covered her with feathery kisses that left her mindless and wanting more. He was a master at love and she was a willing pupil. When he kissed her at the junction of her thighs and moved lower, she knew that if the night had been filled with surprises, there were a few more for her to learn.

Much later, Quinn pushed her hair away from her shoulders and kissed the nape of her neck. "Sara," he said in a lazy voice, "I could get used to this kind of morning."

She sucked in her breath, thinking how much he'd changed and changed her, leaned into his shoulder and thought about the future. A future that would make her life complete, her family whole—a father, a mother, two special children, and, maybe, even more. She cherished the idea, but wondered if Quinn did.

He didn't give her a chance to reply. Brushing her cheeks with gentle hands, he smiled into her eyes. "I guess you'll have to marry me, Sam, or the twins will never forgive you."

"Only the twins?"

"Me, too. Be my woman."

"Whose woman?" she asked, a catch in her throat.

"Mine!" He kissed her into submission.

Sara had dreamed and wished but never thought to hear those words from Quinn. Her heart pounded. "What happened to the angry man with itchy feet who believed in letting tomorrows take care of themselves?"

"That was before I got arrested on a county road and wound up in a town named Juniper." He leaned back into the pillows and drew her over him. "To be honest with you, I fully intended to get lost as soon as I had a chance. But that was before I got to know you and Jase and Katie. I've had a chance to do a lot of thinking in the last few weeks. I realized I've been running for most of my life, headed Lord knows where. But that's over.''

''Are you sure?''

''I'm sure. I'm crazy in love with you, Sam,'' he said, drowning himself in her coffee-colored eyes. ''Will you marry me?''

''Yes, oh yes. I love you, Quinn Tucker.''

When she wrapped her arms around him, he knew that his drifting days were over—and that his life as a husband and a daddy was about to begin.